Prais
Short Stories and H

'A delightful collection of short stories…a generous
selection of tips on improving your writing…ideal for
writers of all abilities.'
Morgen Bailey, novelist, short story writer,
blogger, editor and writing teacher

'If you write – or would like to write – fiction for women's
magazines, this is THE Kindle download
for you.'
Sally Zigmond, novelist and prize-winning short story writer

Praise for
Ghost Stories and How to Write Them

'Spooky stories, spot on advice – I highly
recommend it.'
Della Galton, short story writer, novelist and writing teacher

'A great mix of stories and commentary which between
them will give you all the tools you need to give it a go
yourself. Written in a chatty, no-nonsense style.'
Helen Hunt, short story writer, writing teacher
and Writers' Forum columnist

ISBN-13: 978-1496023858
ISBN-10: 1496023854

This book is also available as an ebook.

Please visit www.kathleenmcgurl.com
for more information and for contact details

Cover image from www.dreamstime.com
Cover design by Connor McGurl
and Chris Callow

Kathleen McGurl

Short Stories

and

How to Write Them

An anthology of women's magazine stories
plus notes on how to write your own

Also by Kathleen McGurl

Ghost Stories and How to Write Them

*An anthology of women's magazine ghost stories
plus notes on how to write your own*

CONTENTS

Introduction	7
What is a Short Story?	8
Different Types of Story	11
Story: High Fliers	13
High Fliers – Discussion	18
Characterisation	19
Point of View	21
Settings	22
Story: On the Road to Katmandu	23
On the Road to Katmandu – Discussion	27
Dialogue	29
Tense	31
Story: Trapped!	33
Trapped! – Discussion	36
Where do you get your ideas?	36
Story: The Fearsome Threesome of Pelham Post Office	39
Fearsome Threesome – Discussion	45
Stewing Time	46
Story: Rosie's Legacy	49
Rosie's Legacy – Discussion	55
Story Structure	55
Story: The Church of Mary O'Reilly	57
Mary O'Reilly – Discussion	61
Check Your Facts	62
Story: Breaking Point	65
Breaking Point – Discussion	72
Editing	73
Story: Queen of the Dawn	77
Queen of the Dawn – Discussion	79
Time to Write	80
Finding Inspiration	82

Story: The Missing Piece   85
The Missing Piece – Discussion   89
Rules of Writing   90
Story: I Don't Know Who To Pick   93
I Don't Know Who to Pick – Discussion   97
Twist Endings   98
Story: The Bet   101
The Bet – Discussion   104
Rejection   104
Story: Finding Mum   107
Finding Mum – Discussion   110
Story: Did I Hit an Angel?   113
Did I Hit an Angel – Discussion   118
Make Good Use of Description   119
Supernatural Stories   119
Other Writers   121
The Ones Which Didn't Sell   122
Story: Acceptance   123
Acceptance – Discussion   128
Story: Aunt Martha's Secrets   131
Aunt Martha's Secrets – Discussion   138
Story: Père Nöel Pops The Question   141
Père Nöel – Discussion   144
Proof-reading   144
Writing Prompts   147
In Conclusion   155
Further Reading   157

Introduction

Hello, and thank you for reading my book! Before we get going, a few words about this book, what's in it and how it is formatted.

This book is a hybrid – part anthology and part How To. It contains sixteen of my stories, most of which have been previously published in women's magazines in the UK and Australia. After each one there's a discussion section in which I talk about my inspiration, and also cover various topics on how to write a good story which, hopefully, will sell to the women's magazine market.

If you're reading this primarily because you like reading short stories, feel free to skip the discussion sections, which are aimed more at writers. If you're a beginner writer, I hope this book will help get you started. If you're a seasoned writer, this book should get you thinking about your stories in a new way, and with luck will provide you with inspiration.

From now on, rather than write 'women's magazines' over and over, I'm going to use the term 'womag' for short. Some readers will already know me as 'womagwriter', via my blog *www.womagwriter.blogspot.co.uk* which is themed around writing short stories for women's magazines, and contains advice and guidelines for writers. Some of the discussion topics in this book borrow from my blog posts – I did not realise I had written so many until I checked back through them while planning this book!

What is a short story?

Let's start by establishing just what is a short story. It must have a beginning, a middle and an end. A successful womag story will start with a character who has a problem (the beginning). During the course of the story, the character needs to resolve the problem, through her own actions. It won't be straightforward and things may get worse (the middle) before they get better and the issue is resolved (the end). By the way, I say 'her' actions, but you can have male main characters as well. Having said that, most published stories tend to involve female main characters. From now on I will refer to 'main character' as 'MC'.

So, your MC starts with a problem, which she resolves, so that by the end of the story she is in a better situation than she was at the beginning. Womag stories DO need to have happy, hopeful or uplifting endings.

Now then, because I've recently read Scarlett Thomas's book, *Monkeys with Typewriters*, (isn't that a great title?) in which she explains story structure, I'm going to pass on a little of my newly acquired knowledge to you, and go on for a bit about Ancient Greeks. Aristotle identified three main types of story – the Epic, the Tragedy and the Comedy. We all know what an Epic is – a long tale with various ups and downs; usually the characters are going on some sort of quest. Think Lord of the Rings. Womag stories are never Epics.

For the difference between Tragedies and Comedies, we're going to have to get a bit mathematical. Before your eyes glaze over, it is very simple, honest! I found it incredibly useful to start thinking of story structure in this way. In a Tragedy, the MC starts out pretty well off, all things considered. Rich, powerful, happy, she's already got what she wants. In the early part of the story, things get better still for this character. But pride comes before a fall, and when things start to go bad they go *really* bad, ending with the MC hitting rock bottom and dying. Either literally (in Shakespeare's historical tragedies) or metaphorically. Here's the maths bit – we can draw a graph of the story arc:

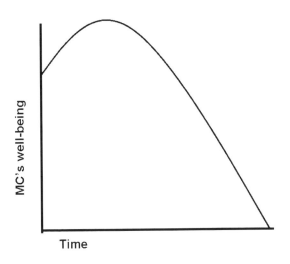

Tragedy Story Arc

I hope you can see that womag stories are never tragedies, either. Earlier I said that in a womag story the MC ends up in a better place than she started from. And *that* is the story arc of a comedy. I don't mean (and neither did Aristotle) comedy as in ha-ha, split your sides laughing.

It's comedy as in a tale with a happy ending. So let's do the maths bit and look at a graph showing the comedy story arc:

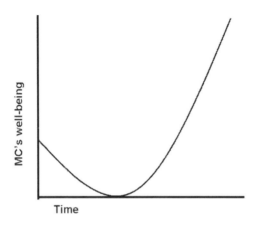

Comedy Story Arc

That's more like it! At the start of the story the MC is low down on the well-being axis – because she has a problem. Things get worse before they get better, but she eventually ends up in a much better state.

Womag stories are *always* comedies, in this sense of the word. Study some, and you'll see this!

Finally, to finish this section, I must unreservedly apologise to anyone who has studied the classics, for what is probably a very poor summary of Aristotle's *Poetics* (which I admit I have never read. I am paraphrasing Scarlett Thomas here.) But this is how I understand it, and thinking about story arc can really help you to structure your writing.

Different Types of Story

I played around for a while trying to categorise the stories I'd picked to include in this section of the book. Of course, there are all sorts of ways to categorise stories. Some of the womag fiction specials classify stories by putting a tag line at the top: 'Spinechiller', 'One from the Heart', 'Moving On', etc. But I've come up with my own method of classification. I realised my stories lay on a spectrum, from farcical humour at one end to tear-jerking emotion at the other. So I've come up with a scale, and have ranked the stories in this book accordingly:

1. Humour – farce. Makes you snigger.
2. Humour – light-hearted. Makes you smile.
3. Family-oriented, sweet. Makes you say 'aw'.
4. Introspective, sad. Makes you think.
5. Emotional. Makes you cry.

When writing a womag story, it's a good idea to have decided up-front where in this scale you are aiming for, even if you don't think of it in quite these terms. Although in a novel you can successfully combine humour with deep emotion, I don't think there is space to do that in a short story, and if you try, you may well end up in a muddle. So decide whether your idea suits a light-hearted tone, or a deeper, heart-rending, soul-searching kind of style, and then stick with that. If a first draft of a story doesn't seem to be working, it may be because you are pitching it at the wrong point of the scale, and changing the tone might make it work better.

Magazines will typically include a mix of stories from all parts of the spectrum. Sometimes fiction editors will publish guidelines or email their known writers, specifically asking for one type of story, in a particular length. If you can write to order, or better still, already have a stock of different types, you will give yourself a great chance of being published.

Anyway, I've had a go at classifying all the stories included in this book, using the above scale. But I'm not going to tell you how I classified them, until after each story. As you read through, see where *you* think each story sits, and at the end, we'll see whether you and I agree. Some, I think, are clear cut and very obviously fit into one of my categories. Others are more debatable. And have a think about your own stories – are they more towards one end of the scale or the other? Are there categories you shy away from writing and categories you love writing best? Or are your stories better classified in some other way? Remember, this is just my scale, invented to fit around the stories I'd already chosen for this book. There's no right or wrong here, just opinion.

OK, I think it's time for a story. We'll kick off with one I would rate as a very typical womag story, if there is such a thing. It was first published in *My Weekly* back in 2007.

High Fliers

'She's just so embarrassing, Mum,' said Claire. I swallowed a sigh. So were you at her age, I wanted to say. Instead I poured out two cups of tea, and handed one to her.

'Thanks. She's pierced her belly button. Did I tell you that already?' Claire went on, grimacing.

'You did. I suppose it's the fashion, these days…' I must admit, it wasn't something I'd do, but then I'm not sixteen, like my lovely granddaughter Kirsty. I sat down opposite Claire at my kitchen table.

'But it's horrible! And she wears low-slung jeans with cropped tops to show it off.'

'She has a great figure. I don't blame her for wanting to make the most of it. I'd wear those clothes and show my midriff if it wasn't so baggy.'

'Mum!' Claire tut-tutted and turned away from me. She took a prim sip of her tea. I'd shocked her. Good. Sometimes she could be a bit, how would Kirsty put it? Up herself.

'Seriously, Mum. I can't talk to her these days. When she was little we used to be so close. We had wonderful times dressing her dolls and making little fairy cakes. I know I can't keep her like that forever, but I wish we could find something we'd enjoy doing together again.'

'What about a shopping trip?' I'd go shopping with

Kirsty like a shot if she asked me. What a fabulous excuse to go round Top Shop and Miss Selfridge, with a trendy teenager. The shop assistants all look sideways at me if I go in alone. I'm far too old and frumpy, I suppose I spoil their image.

'Absolutely not. I'd spend hours standing outside the changing rooms holding her bags while she tried on everything in the shop. And I'd get *nothing* for myself because she refuses to set foot in M&S.' Claire shook her head.

And *you'd* refuse to go in *her* favourite shops, I thought. I'd have to think of something different to pull them together. 'What did we do together when you were a teenager?'

'Can't remember much. I used to go to the roller disco every week when I was Kirsty's age. You would drop me off and pick me up.'

'Yes, I remember.' I also recall despairing at how tight your jeans were, and wondering why you insisted on crimping your hair in that hideous style.

'But what did we do together?' Claire stirred her tea thoughtfully. 'Oh yes, we planted sunflower seeds.'

'Did we?'

'Yes, one summer. And we raced them to see whose would grow tallest – the high fliers, we called them. That was fun. I love sunflowers.'

Fun, in a way, perhaps. But not a great way to get two headstrong women, the twin hearts of my world, my own high fliers, communicating again. I'd have to mull it over.

Kirsty called in the next day on her way home from school. She dropped her bag in the hallway, kicked off her boots and threw herself face down onto my sofa.

I put a cup of coffee beside her, strong and black just

as she liked it. 'Had a good day, love?'

'Not really,' she replied, her voice muffled by a cushion. 'Jazz is trying to organise a girls' shopping trip to London in half term. But I bet Mum won't let me go. She's so uncool, it's embarrassing. All my friends' mums will let them go. You'd have let me, too, if you were my mum, wouldn't you?'

'Hold on, hold on,' I said. 'Have you actually asked her yet?'

'Not as such. But I know what she'll say.' She looked up at me. Her frown was so deep you could have grown potatoes in her forehead.

'Try her, you might be surprised.'

'I can't talk to her, Gran. As soon as I open my mouth she puts this disapproving look on her face, like she's swallowed a lemon. She went ape when I showed her my belly button. Look, d'you want to see it?' She flipped herself over onto her back, and hoisted up her jumper. A delicate little diamante stud nestled in the side of her tummy button.

'Looks lovely, sweetheart. Mind you keep it clean, though.'

'I knew you'd like it! You understand me so much better than Mum. She drives me mad.' She twisted round on the sofa, putting her legs up on the back and letting her head hang down over the edge. It didn't look comfortable.

She sighed and stretched out her arms. 'Sometimes I wish I could turn into a bird. A big one – an eagle or something. I'd fly high up in the sky, circling our house. I'd squawk a goodbye to Mum, then I'd be off, away to my mountaintop nesting site, where I could do whatever I want…'

'You'd miss your friends. And anyway, birds don't have belly buttons to put diamante studs in.'

She threw a cushion at me for that. But she'd given me an idea.

On Saturday at ten to two I stood on the heath land beside the Hungry Hikers café, wondering which of them would be first to arrive. Claire was coming from home, Kirsty from her friend's house nearby, both reluctant. Neither of them knew what I was planning for them.

I'd spent hours trying to think of something they could enjoy doing together. It had to be an activity new to both of them, on neutral ground, something which would allow them to talk if they wanted, or just be together if they didn't feel ready to talk. Then Kirsty's fantasy about flying had put the idea into my head…

Kirsty arrived first. She trudged across the heath towards me, shoulders hunched, hands deep in her jeans pockets.

'Hi Gran. What are we doing? Not walking, I hope. It's too windy.'

'Hello love. No, we're not walking. Ah, here's your mother.' I'd spotted Claire's red car pulling into the café car park. A minute later she was with us. I suppressed a chuckle at the way her hands were thrust into her coat pockets, pushing her shoulders up. Really, they were so alike, these two. They had so much in common, deep down. If only they'd let themselves see it, they'd soon be each other's best friend.

'Hello, Mum. Hi, Kirsty. What's this all about, then?' They looked at me with identical questioning brown eyes.

'One for you,' I said, pulling a package out of my bag, and handing it to Kirsty. 'And one for you.' They frowned, and looked at what I'd given them.

'A kite! Hey that's, um, cool!' Kirsty was first to rip open the packaging. She sat down on the ground and began to put it together.

'A kite? Whatever for?' asked Claire.

'To fly, of course!' squealed Kirsty. 'Thanks, Gran! Come on, let's see who can get theirs in the air first. Wow, mine's in the shape of a bird. What's yours?'

Claire was smiling now, as she hurried to insert the rods and attach the strings. 'Some kind of flower, oh how lovely, it's a sunflower! Bet mine'll fly higher than yours!'

'No way! Gran, help us launch them?'

It took a while, but soon we had both kites up in the air. An eagle and a sunflower, flying high and proud. I went back to the café and sat at an outside table to watch. Claire and Kirsty stood side by side, sometimes chatting, sometimes laughing, sometimes just watching the kites.

As I watched, Claire's kite crossed suddenly in front of Kirsty's, then the two sets of strings wound themselves around and around each other, and the kites dived inevitably towards the ground. I got up to go and help re-launch them, but stopped as Claire and Kirsty, laughing, hugged each other in the middle of the heath, their arms as entangled as their kite strings.

I pulled a tissue out of my pocket. Must have been the strong wind that'd made my eyes water.

The End

High Fliers – Discussion

Before reading on, have a think about where on my scale you would put this story. In case you've forgotten (already!) the categories are:

1. Humour – farce. Makes you snigger.
2. Humour – light-hearted. Makes you smile.
3. Family-oriented, sweet. Makes you say 'aw'.
4. Introspective, sad. Makes you think.
5. Emotional. Makes you cry.

The ending is uplifting, and I hope it left you with a smile. You can see it follows the comedy story arc – the MC has a problem in that her beloved daughter and grand-daughter just don't seem to get on. It's a typical generational difference – the teenager thinks her mum's boring and old-fashioned, and the mother is upset by her mildly rebellious offspring. It takes the older, wiser, seen-it-all-before grandmother, who has that little bit more distance, to bring them back together. This family don't have real problems, just mild niggles. All of which should help you put it into the same category I did – category 3.

Readers who aren't well acquainted with the UK womags might raise an eyebrow at Kirsty's belly-button piercing. Are such things allowed in these magazines? Well, yes, this story was published. But better than that – when emailing me to accept this story, the fiction editor praised it for its contemporary feel. I wanted to make Kirsty seem like a real teenager from today, so the belly-button piercing was important as something which would upset her mother (in my day, it'd have been a second ear piercing). I also had her hooking her legs onto the back of the sofa and hanging her head down. (I did this myself to check it was possible without slithering off and banging your head on the floor. I don't recommend the position.)

Characterisation

If womag stories start with a character who has a problem, it follows that characterisation is one of the most important things to get right in these stories. So it's a good idea if we discuss this aspect of womag story writing first. Your characters must seem alive, feel as though they could step off the page and come to sit next to you on the sofa, reading over your shoulder. (*'Hey, I'd never do that! What, sit quietly and read a story from one of Mum's boring magazines? No way!'* Ahem. That's enough, Kirsty. We've finished with your story now and I'm talking about characters in more general terms.)

So, how do you create real, believable characters? One obvious way is to base them on people you know. But we don't all have suitable templates to hand. I've only got teenage sons, no daughters. However, I used to be a teenage girl, back in the eighties, and I can remember those conflicts with my own mother all too well. And I have friends with teenage girls whom they love to bits but sometimes despair of. So you put it all together into a big mixing pot, give it a stir and hopefully out will pop a character. Sometimes they arrive fully formed. Other times they're shy and need a bit of coaxing before you find out who they really are. On those occasions, a character sheet might help.

There are character sheets available online, but I would advise compiling your own. Simply write a list of questions you feel you should know about your character. Begin with the obvious ones, eg name, age, appearance, occupation, to get you in the mood. Then add some more interesting ones such as:

- What is your earliest childhood memory?
- What frightens you most?
- What did you dream of last night?
- What would be your perfect day out?
- Who annoys you most in your family?
- What's your greatest ambition?
- What makes you laugh?

The questions can be anything which helps you get under the character's skin. Then imagine you are interviewing your character for a Sunday supplement. Let them answer in their own words – use first person (I remember… I am frightened of…), even if you plan to write your story in third person point of view (she did this, he said that). First person point of view at this stage helps you get right inside your character's head.

You might feel it is overkill to fill in a character sheet for every character for a 1000-word story, and perhaps it is. But it is probably worth doing one for the main characters in every story. And you never know, when your character reveals what frightens them the most, or what their ultimate ambition is, you may very well find you have material for not one but several stories, featuring the same character.

Kirsty and her mother Claire have certainly appeared in more than one of my stories. The more you write about the same characters, the better you get to know them, and the more real they will seem. I know a novelist whose MC became so real she ended up with her own Twitter account and Facebook page. She also tried to gate-crash her own book launch.

Once you've got to know your character, be careful

not to include a huge wodge of description which regurgitates your character sheet. Instead, try dropping in bits and pieces throughout your story, so that by the end the reader has a good idea of who they are. And remember, actions speak louder than words, so have your characters *do* something which *shows* their character, rather than telling the reader what they're like.

Author Alison MacLeod, in an essay included in *Short Circuit: A Guide to the Art of the Short Story*, described a short story as 'the *unfolding* of a character'. I think this is an excellent way of thinking of short stories. In novels you can include acres of plot, reams of description and piles of poetic language if you so desire. But there's no room for that in a short story. There's only room for one or two main characters, and you must unfold them quickly and efficiently, ensuring the reader feels an intimacy with them as soon as possible. When your character starts telling *you* what they want to do and say, and you're simply typing or scribbling as fast as you can several steps behind – that's when you know you've created someone real.

Point of View

Once you've decided upon your characters, you next need to determine what point of view to use. There are two things to consider here: firstly, whose point of view to use (could be one or more than one of your characters) and secondly, whether to use first or third person.

Whose point of view – this is best decided by considering whose story it is. Which of your characters has most to lose, or most to gain? If you're the kind of writer who starts with a character then there's rarely any debate about whose point of view to use. But if you have started with a plot idea rather than a character, you may need to think about this for a while. Sometimes a story needs to be written from the point of view of several characters. This is fine as long as you limit the number of viewpoint characters, and ensure you don't 'head-hop' – each scene should use only one point of view.

First or third person – if you're intending using more than one point of view in your story you'll probably be best using third person (he said…, she did…). But if your entire story will be from a single character's point of view, you have a choice between using third or first person. Using first person (I did… I said…) often helps you get into your character's head, but some magazines prefer stories in third person. Some writers feel more comfortable using one or the other. If you're not sure, pick one at random. It's surprisingly easy (if a little tedious) to switch to the other if you decide later you've made the wrong decision.

Settings

Right then, for a womag story, we've established we need a good, strong character, and we've chosen a point of view. We also need a setting, and an unusual setting will certainly help to sell a story. Have a look at this next story as an example. It's one of my favourites, and I'll tell you why, after you've read it.

On the Road to Katmandu

I've been on the bus about four hours – time mostly spent staring out of the window – when I lift my hand from where it's been resting on my leg. It leaves a clear imprint. This dust gets everywhere.

We're climbing steadily, up into the Himalayan foothills. I thought the air would be clearer up here, but the sky is still that murky pink colour, and if you breathe deeply the airborne dust will make you cough. Ironic, really. I came here to feel renewed.

The bus is packed – every seat filled with local people. And more men above, clinging on to the roof, on which my rucksack is precariously strapped. There are animals on board too – a couple of dogs, some chickens and a small goat.

There are great views across the valley, but I've also seen sights I'd rather not have. A truck, tumbled off the side of the road, twisted and broken at the bottom. A burnt out car. And most worryingly of all, a bus, like the one I'm in, lying in a tangled mess half way down the valley side.

I look away. There are some things it is better not to think about. Like what I've left behind me, back in England.

Across the aisle from me there's another Westerner. He got on at the last stop, twenty minutes back. He wears the standard uniform of the hippy traveller – baggy faded trousers, flip-flops, t-shirt from Bangkok and a grubby cotton braid tied around his left wrist. His hair is dirty blond, and he clearly hasn't shaved for weeks. He grins at me. His eyes are friendly.

'Don't worry. I've done this trip a few times and never gone over the edge. Not *yet*, anyway.' He winks, then immediately looks mortified. 'Oh, God, sorry. Your expression – you really are nervous, aren't you?'

'Well, just a bit,' I say. 'It does look like there's been a lot of accidents on this road. And this bus is ancient – what if it breaks down or has a blow-out or something? If the driver lost control…'

I'm babbling. He laughs. 'Hey, tell you what. Talk to me and I'll take your mind off it. So, what's your name, where are you from, the usual. Or better still, cut all that and just tell me what you're looking for?' His accent is southern English, with a hint of Australian, as though he's spent the last few months down under.

'My name's Cally. From London. What do you mean – what am I looking for?'

'Hi, Cally, I'm Jez.' He leans across and shakes my hand, oddly formal. A chicken runs up the aisle between us. 'Everyone who comes here is looking for something. Close your eyes, Cally.'

I do, and lean back in my seat.

'Now, what are you looking for? First word which comes into your head.'

'Safety,' I say. My choice of word could have had something to do with the way the bus lurched around a particularly tight hairpin at that moment.

'Safety, hmm. So you're running away? From something, or someone?'

Someone. Someone I once thought I loved.

I laugh. 'Not running away. I don't do that – I'm Strong. I'm a Strong Independent Woman.' I didn't mean to say it with capital letters. But that's been my mantra since I left, and it's the way I see those words in my mind.

'So, Strong Independent Cally, you've travelled all the way from London to seek safety in Katmandu? Yet you're running from nothing. Hmm.'

'Why do you think I'm running away?'

'Because, dear Cally, you have the look of an escaped convict. Who was he, anyway?'

I jump, startled, then try to disguise it by shifting position in the torn, uncomfortable seat. A protruding nail catches the back of my knee, scratching me through my trousers.

He was my fiancé. Until I realised he wanted an ornament, not a partner. He'd wooed me with flowers, expensive dinners, then jewels. I'd been smitten.

But I need to lighten the tone here, before I start telling this stranger my life history. Asia does that to you. You only need know a fellow traveller five minutes before you share your most intimate details with them. I guess your guard's down, because you figure you'll never see them again, after the few days during which your paths cross.

'He?' I giggle and raise my eyebrows. 'Might have been a *she*.' Maybe it'd be fun to flirt with this guy, a little. There's nothing and no one to stop me.

Jez sits back, looks me up and down thoughtfully and shakes his head. 'No, it was definitely a he. What did he do that was so bad?'

Now he's annoying me with his mind-reading. I look away from him, out of the window. Maybe worrying about going over the edge isn't so bad after all. But this journey is twelve hours long, and we're less than half way. So I'd better try to get on with him.

'He told me,' I say, leaning across the aisle conspiratorially, 'that I was fat, ugly, and boring.'

Jez guffaws. He has a good, hearty laugh. The kind you want to hear again.

'You're skinny enough to be a size zero, you have looks to die for, and how can anyone who takes a bus to Katmandu be boring? Try again, beautiful Cally.'

He suffocated me. He tried to mould me into the trophy wife he wanted. He destroyed my dreams and stunted my growth. I became his Bonsai tree – something small, beautiful and manicured, but above all, limited.

I think for a moment. 'He poisoned me,' I say. 'He put deadly nightshade into a salad. I was in hospital for months while they got the poison out of my system. That's why I'm so thin.'

'But with a healthy glow in your cheeks,' laughs Jez. 'And such a mischievous glint in your eye. Next!'

I try to look serious. 'He ran off with my best friend. And my dog. And my cat and my collection of tadpoles.'

'Hmm, that'd annoy anyone. Except he'd be welcome to the tadpoles. But you're the one running, not him. Still don't believe you.'

'He clipped my wings, docked my tail, espaliered me to fit his idea of the perfect woman.'

'Horrible mixed metaphors there, but I think we're somewhere near the truth.' Jez smiles at me and reaches for my hand. He rubs it gently with his thumb, making a sweaty circle in the dust. 'What you and I both need, grubby Cally, is a shower.'

He's not wrong there. 'That's the first thing I intend doing in Katmandu, Jez. I want a decent hotel, no more cheap backpackers' lodges. One with an en-suite bathroom and fully tiled shower. I'll stand under the water for at least an hour until I look like a prune.'

'Ah, wrinkly Cally, I can do better than that. Stay till next month. The monsoon's due, and this place is unbelievable after the rain. Everything sparkles like diamonds, it's clear and cool. The rain washes all the dust from the air and you can see for miles. Like the whole country gets a bath. It cleans, purifies and allows everything to grow again. It's amazing.'

I'd be washed clean of my past. I'd be able to grow and move on, instead of crashing to the bottom of life's valley like those trucks back there.

I smile at Jez, and nod. Strong, independent, clean Cally.

I gently remove my hand from his clasp. Now I know what I'm looking for.

Freedom.

The End

On the Road to Katmandu – Discussion

A bus winding its way up through the Himalayan foothills on the way to the Nepalese capital – yep, that's an unusual setting all right, and one which I think went a long way towards selling this story, to *My Weekly* in 2009. It might not surprise you to hear that I've travelled in such a bus complete with loose chickens in the aisle, and so the setting was described largely from memory. As with many of my stories I can remember the genesis of this one. My online writing group at that time were holding monthly competitions, to write a story using a single word prompt. The prompt that month was 'dust'. I could remember all too well that choking pre-monsoon dust, and the handprint

Cally left on her leg came from my own experience. And so I began with a girl on a Nepalese bus.

Good settings help to sell stories, without a doubt. So next time you sit your characters down in a kitchen drinking coffee while they have the important conversation they need to have to move the story forward, stop and think. Why a kitchen? Why drink coffee? Yes, it's probably true to life, but this is fiction, and you're allowed to make things up. Make them have their conversation somewhere entirely different. While out jogging in the rain. While maintaining a tricky yoga pose. While trying on wetsuits. While queuing for Wimbledon tickets. The world's your oyster.

If you analyse *On the Road to Katmandu*, you'll quickly realise there's very little plot in it. Let's list what actually happens in the story: Cally's on a bus, Cally talks to Jez. That's it. Not a lot, really. But there's plenty of back story, told as Cally's thoughts rather than as flashback.

When writing this story, I began with no real feel for where it was going. That's unusual for me. I know many writers start with an image, an idea, or a snippet of dialogue and let the story unfold as they write it, but I prefer to have an ending in mind before I begin. Here, I vaguely thought that it would end with a hint that Cally would get together with fellow traveller Jez. I clearly didn't know Cally well enough. Hadn't done a character sheet for her. Jez started out as a 'type', and anyone who's travelled on the cheap in the far east or Africa or South America, will probably recognise him to some extent. Part way through writing it, Cally began to come alive for me. Eventually, as I neared the end, she left the page, sat beside me and said, '*Please* tell me you're not going to pair me off with Jez? He's nice, but beginning to irritate.' She had a point. I realised she deserved better, after escaping from that restrictive relationship with Bonsai-man. And so I gave her freedom. She smiled, happy with the ending. As I hope you did, when reading it.

I'd classify this one as a 4 – introspective, makes you think. What category did you put it in?

I promised I'd tell you why it's one of my favourites. Well, because of the comment I had from the *My Weekly* fiction editor when she bought the story. If you don't mind me blowing my own trumpet for a moment here: she described the story as 'lovely, lovely, lovely, and quietly sophisticated'. Makes me grin stupidly every time I think of that comment. If no one else ever says anything nice about my writing, I'll still have that to hold on to when I'm old and grey. Feedback is *so* important.

Dialogue

There's not a lot of plot in *On the Road to Katmandu*, but there's certainly plenty of dialogue. In fact, it's almost all dialogue, interspersed with Cally's thoughts, and a few snippets of action, such as the chicken running up the aisle. I would suggest that including dialogue is *essential* for womag stories. At least one fiction editor (*Woman's Weekly*) has been quoted as saying she'd be unlikely to buy a story which contained no dialogue at all.

Why is that? Probably because nothing brings characters to life more than putting words in their mouths. Also, dialogue helps with pace – the plot moves along more quickly when characters are talking, rather than when the author is describing things. And it looks better on the page. All those lovely indents and short snippets of speech leaving plenty of white space create a more inviting and easier to read page than big heavy blocks of text.

So it's vitally important to make your dialogue sound natural and realistic. By that I don't mean you should mimic exactly the roundabout, waffly way many of us speak (or is it just me?) Rather, you need to condense it down, ensure your characters are concise and precise when they speak, yet still have them only use words and phrases people actually do use when speaking. It might take a bit of practice, and the dialogue sections of your stories may well be the parts needing most editing, but the work will pay off.

You can bring out character through speech as well. Maybe have someone use a particular speech pattern (Jez uses Cally's name a lot, prefixed by various adjectives) but don't overdo it or it'll become annoying (unless you *want* the character to come across as irritating! Jez crossed the line about two thirds of the way through). You can portray a character's age, education, nationality, regionality and social class through dialogue by choosing their words carefully.

However, bear in mind at all times that *less is more*. Never put in too much dialect (*eee by gum, does tha belly touch tha bum?* said the Yorkshireman, and there's a joke lost on my non-British readers) but a little bit in the right places can help. Consider having your northern (English) character say 'I'll not...' instead of the more southern 'I won't...' Your teenager might exclaim 'Awesome!' whereas her mother will say 'Great!' and her grandfather, 'Splendid!'. 'There's lovely,' said the Welshman. 'Sure and what will you be writing about next?' asked the Irishman. 'Och, aye, another wee story,' said the Scot.

But do be careful not to let your characters become stereotypes.

Tense

Did you notice that *On the Road to Katmandu* is written in present tense (Jez says, I think, etc) rather than past tense (Jez said, I thought, etc)? Present tense can make a story seem more immediate — the reader is *there* with the main character and experiencing the events alongside them. Personally I think present tense works well with first-person point of view, but can seem strained and awkward when used in a third-person story. As with point of view, experiment and see which works best for each story. But beware — some magazine editors won't publish present tense stories. As always, research your market before submitting. It's tedious but not difficult to edit a story to switch from one to the other.

Time for another story. Let's lighten the tone. This next story is very short, just 700 words, and is also heavily dependent on dialogue. Originally published in *My Weekly*.

Trapped!

'Where are the Post-its, Carol?' called Anne.

'In the cupboard, bottom shelf on the left,' I replied.

'Can't see them.'

I sighed and hauled myself to my feet. Geoff, the third member of our little team at Holland's Copy Shop, sniggered. Of course, he wouldn't lift a finger to help. If you want something done get Carol to do it. Good old Carol, she always has time to help. No matter that I had a 10 o'clock coming up with Miss Smolenski, the client from hell.

The stationery cupboard was long and narrow, with a tiny window at the far end, and rows of shelves along both sides. Anne was peering helplessly at the top shelf. I went in and grabbed a pack of Post-its from the bottom shelf.

'Here you are,' I said.

'And here you two are, my lovelies!' chuckled Geoff as he entered the cupboard and pulled the door closed behind him.

'Don't be an idiot, Geoff. I'm not in the mood for this and I've got Miss Smolenski, the client from hell, at ten,' I snapped.

'Aw Carol, it's just a bit of fun. I'm not stopping you leaving.'

No, apart from having to push past him. The

cupboard is only one person wide. Predictably, Geoff wriggled and raised his eyebrows suggestively as I squeezed past.

I reached the door and turned the handle. It went round uselessly, then came off in my hand.

'Now look what you've done,' I said.

'Let me try,' said Geoff. 'Your gallant knight to the rescue!' We went through the squeeze and wriggle routine again to swap places. But he couldn't get the handle back on. The spindle had worked its way inside the door.

Anne was looking pale. 'Carol, dear, I'm getting a little hot. I never did like confined spaces.'

She was right – it was becoming pretty uncomfortable. Large patches of sweat were appearing on Geoff's shirt. 'Open the window,' I said, fanning my face. 'And for goodness sake, nobody break wind.'

'Look,' said Geoff. 'I've found a golf club.' He pulled a pitching wedge from the top shelf and began swinging it at the door.

'Ow, be careful!' I yelled, as his backswing caught me round the ear. The club made no impression on the door at all.

'We'll have to shout, and hope someone hears,' I said decisively. 'Help! Help!'

'Ssh,' whispered Anne. 'Someone's come into the office. I heard the door. We've got a customer.'

I looked at my watch. Two minutes to ten. It could be Miss Smolenski, the client from hell.

We all held our breath.

Footsteps paced the floor, fingers drummed on a desk, a woman's voice muttered crossly, and several epochs later the office door opened, banged shut, and there was silence.

We all let out our breath.

'Whoever that was could have let us out,' Geoff said.

'So why didn't you shout?' I retorted.

'Why didn't you?'

We all looked sheepishly at our feet.

'Let me get to the door,' said Anne. She was nearest the window so had to push past both of us. 'Anyone got any pliers?'

'Well of course,' I said. 'I've an entire tool kit in my handbag, *out there.'*

'I mean, are there any in here?'

There weren't. But there was, incongruously, a large pair of fish tweezers. 'They'll do,' said Anne, pouncing on them. I was amazed. She's usually so helpless, but here she was taking charge.

With the tweezers, she managed to grasp the spindle and pull it through. She slotted the handle back into place, turned it, and we were out.

'Thank God!' said Geoff, wiping the sweat from his forehead. 'I'm sorry. That's the last time I play a joke like that.'

I smiled at him, just grateful to be out from under his armpit. I noticed a scribbled note on my desk, and read it quickly.

'Miss Smolenski, the client from hell! It *was* her who came in, she's gone for a coffee and will be back at 10.20. She's not happy.'

We looked at our watches. 10.19. Footsteps approached outside the office. With one accord, we all dived for the stationery cupboard and slammed the door shut behind us.

Phew.

The End

Trapped! – Discussion

Clearly a category one story – total farce. I must tell you the story behind the story here, as it's almost as good as the story itself. I was on a packed commuter train to London one morning, and a pair of women who were obviously off on a shopping trip were sitting opposite me, chatting and giggling. After a while I began to tune in to their conversation, and caught the tail end of a hilarious story, something about being trapped in a cupboard at work. I wished I'd heard the whole thing. Then they got talking to a nice-looking fella who was standing beside us, and they offered to squeeze up together to give him a bit of space to sit down, three to a double seat. I saw my chance.

'You want to watch those two,' I told him. 'They've been telling each other hilarious stories. That one about being stuck in the cupboard, go on, tell him!'

The ladies obliged, repeating the entire story with some embellishment as they warmed to their audience. This time I listened closely, and we all laughed uproariously at the end. As we got off the train, I told the ladies I was a writer, and would write up that anecdote for a magazine – at which they squealed and laughed even more. *Trapped!* was the resulting story. I wonder if they ever saw it in print?

Where do you get your ideas from?

Every writer I know has been asked that question, dozens of times, by non-writers. One writer says she always answers that she gets them from the ideas shop on the corner, where they sell them for a pound a dozen. I get mine from anywhere and everywhere, and as you've just seen, I'll happily use an overheard conversation as the inspiration for a story. I find humorous stories the hardest to make up from scratch, so if there's a funny anecdote I can use as the basis of the story that's all for the good.

I should mention here that there is a difference between a story and an anecdote, and it's an important difference. An anecdote says, 'this happened' and that's it. A story says, 'this happened, these characters changed as a result, and maybe you the reader will now think differently about this.' In other words, a story has a *point* to make, a message to get across, whereas an anecdote doesn't. *Trapped!* is unusual as a published story, in that it is really just an anecdote. I was aware of this when writing it, and tried to get some character change going on – Geoff apologises, ineffectual Anne turns out to be the one who gets them out of their predicament. Perhaps there's a bit of a message in there too – something about how a crisis brings out the best in people – but I think that's probably stretching it a little. With very short humorous tales, you can just about get away with writing anecdotes.

So what do you do if you have a great anecdote but think it probably isn't enough on its own? You need to add layers, develop characters, and try to come up with a universal truth the story can illustrate. But be careful not to force it – *Trapped!* would be a weaker story if I'd tried to drum home the message about rising to meet a crisis. An alternative treatment for humour is to mix and match – pile more and more comedy moments on top of each other. If you have two or three anecdotes which alone aren't enough, try combining them into one story. That's what I did when writing the next story, which was originally published in *The Weekly News*.

The Fearsome Threesome
of Pelham Post Office

Everyone in our village knows it's next to impossible to get money out of the Post Office. Your own money, I mean. The three old biddies who work there are so terrifying many people won't even try to withdraw their money. There's Doris Wright, Beatrice Saunders, and the scariest of all, Mrs Poole. No one knows her first name, and no one, not even Doris and Beatrice, are brave enough to ask.

Here's what happened last time I needed to get some money out. I tried to sneak in quietly, but there's a nerve-jangling bell attached to the door. The three ladies looked sternly at me. I'd disturbed them from their money counting, form sorting and envelope stacking, or whatever it is they find to do so busily whenever a teenager appears. (I think they'd lock us all up, given half a chance.) When they saw who I was they sighed, shook their heads and muttered to each other, then returned to what they were doing.

I chose Beatrice Saunders' counter to stand politely in front of, because she's marginally less fearsome than Doris Wright. (If the worst happens, and only Mrs Poole is on duty, you simply turn around and leave, hoping she hasn't noticed you.) I waited five minutes while Bea finished refilling her stapler, then smiled in what I hoped was a friendly, confident and grown-up fashion, but which probably made me look like a schoolboy caught smoking behind the bike shed.

Finally she looked up. 'Yes?'

I quivered. 'I'd like to withdraw a hundred pounds from my savings account, please.'

'A hundred?' Her eyebrows went up. 'Whatever for?'

I had to tell the truth. If I didn't, she'd find out anyway, and next time would be worse. 'I'm in a band at college, Mrs Saunders. With Gary and Adam. I'm the bass player, and I need to buy a guitar. Second hand.'

'A guitar? Does your mother know you're here, young Simon Armitage?'

'Yes, she said it was ok. Anyway,' I continued foolishly, 'I am eighteen now, and…'

'Oh, *eighteen* are you now? Old enough to know what you want to do with your money? Is it your money, or is it the money your poor, hard-working mother put aside for you each week while you were growing up?'

I cringed. I'd set her off, and knew from past experience I could either just leave now or stay and face the onslaught if I really wanted my cash.

'I suppose you don't have a job? No. Of course not. You young things just think life's one long game. Isn't that right, Doris?'

'Tis indeed, Beatrice. No sense of duty or responsibility, this generation. In our day, lads of his age would be bringing home a pay-packet every week, saving as much as they could, not buying – what is it the boy wants, Beatrice?'

'A *guitar*, Doris.'

'An electric one,' I added, immediately kicking myself.

Their lips pursed simultaneously, and they shook their

heads. I could see Mrs Poole in the back room, and just prayed she couldn't hear the conversation. If she joined in too, I knew I'd lose my nerve and run. And I did need that guitar.

It's not just me, they're like this with anyone under the age of fifty. My Granddad loves them, though. Says they're always really nice and chatty when he goes in for his pension. I just wish there was a cash-point in Pelham.

So when I needed to take £600 from my savings account to buy my first car, you can understand why it took me three weeks to pluck up the courage to go in there. By that time, the guy selling the car was getting pretty annoyed that I hadn't yet turned up with the money. He wanted to re-advertise the car, sell it to someone else. I had to beg him to hang on for me.

I picked my moment carefully. Chose a time when I knew Mrs Poole would be out, having her weekly café lunch with her sister. And, I took our dog, Sally, with me. Don't know why, I mean she's hardly a guard dog, the big old softie, but somehow having her beside me gave me confidence. I pushed the door open gently, even though I knew the bell would jangle. But it didn't – and I saw why when I got inside.

They were having some work done. The bell had been removed while the door was being painted. All the greetings cards fixtures had been pushed to one side of the shop, and there was a polythene sheet covering the counter. Decorators' dust sheets covered the floor, and a tray of paint was balanced precariously on an upturned bucket. Typical that the ladies wouldn't shut up shop while the work was going on, or even get it done after hours. They'd want to be closely supervising every last paint-stroke. I didn't envy the poor decorators.

'You, boy!' Doris's voice thundered across the room. 'Keep your dog well away from that paint! And don't touch that wall, it's wet. What do you want, anyway?'

'Well, I…' I began. Beatrice appeared from the back room.

'Oh, you again, Simon Armitage. Did you waste all that money on a guitar, then? Suppose you want a drum kit now. Get that dog away from the paint!'

I looked around for somewhere Sally could sit and wait. She's well-behaved; she'll sit where I tell her. Behind the greetings cards fixtures looked good. Actually I felt I'd like to cower there myself for a while.

I was just settling Sally down when the door burst open again. From where I was, behind the fixture, I couldn't see what happened next but I could hear everything.

A voice, youngish and male, shouted at the ladies. Shouted! Good grief, he must have been very brave or very stupid, I thought.

'Everyone get down on the floor! Face down, arms spread. This is a hold-up! Get on the floor, NOW!'

I could hear Beatrice and Doris muttering. Give them their due, they didn't scream. I stayed crouched down, holding tight onto Sally's collar and wondered what to do.

'I said, on the floor, NOW! And that means you!' He must have pointed at Doris – it was her voice which answered.

'Don't you point that thing at me, young man. I'd lie on the floor if I could, but you see, I have angina. If I get down there I'm sure I'd never get up again. And you want me face down? Listen, my lad, that's the worst thing to do in my condition. I'd have a heart attack, and then you'd have murder on your hands. It's one thing to be put away for armed robbery but quite another for murder, you know.

Look, I've got my hands on my head. That will have to do.'

'You, then,' the fellow said, sounding a little less confident. 'You, down on the floor, now!'

When Beatrice spoke she sounded old and shaky, quite unlike her usual strident tones.

'Oh, Doris dear, I don't know what to do! This young man wants me to lie down on the floor. But if I do that, I'm sure it'll do for my varicose veins. What should I do, Doris? Do you think I could do it if I got down slowly? I'm afraid one will burst, and there'd be blood everywhere.'

'Oh, Beatrice, no. I don't think you should lie on the floor, not with your veins. Perhaps ask him, dear, if it's ok to just put your hands on your head like I've done?'

'Hands on head, then. Do it!'

'Oh, but the thing is, that'll drain the blood from my arms,' Beatrice went on. 'If I put my arms up, the blood all drains down into my legs, and makes the veins worse. I don't want to be difficult, but I'd be sure to burst one if I put my hands on my head. I'll put them here, on the counter where you can see them.'

'OK, and don't move! Now, give me the money, all of it!'

'Doris, does he mean me to give him the money? Only if I'm not to move, I don't quite see how I can?'

'You can move, but only to do what I tell you. No tricks, all right? Open that till.'

'Beatrice dear, open your till for the young man,' said Doris.

I could hear her fumbling with keys as she opened it. 'Are you sure you want this one opened? Only we've not been using this one today. There's no money in it.'

'Open the other one then, bitch!' Oh no. Big mistake. Seems he was more stupid than brave, after all. You don't swear at these ladies, and you certainly don't call them names. I could feel them bristle from twenty feet away.

'Listen young man,' said Doris. 'There's no need for that sort of behaviour. A little politeness wouldn't go amiss, you know. In my day, young people were brought up to respect their elders, weren't they, Beatrice?'

'Oh yes, Doris. Even in this sort of situation.'

Well, I was riveted. I was dying to know what would happen next, but Sally chose just that moment to sneeze.

The robber swore. 'Who else is in here? Come out! Walk out slowly with your hands up.'

Oh no. That magic word, 'walk'. Sally woofed, and wagging her tail madly, ran out from behind the fixture. She bounded around the shop, barking happily. Too late I remembered the paint tray, and went out to try to stop her knocking it over. But worse had happened. She'd swept her tail across the tray, and was now wagging paint all over the shop. Over the robber too – he was now splattered all over with a delicate shade of duck egg blue. That was enough for him. He made for the door, and reached it at the same moment as Mrs Poole, returning from her lunch break.

I'm not sure if I've mentioned it already, but Mrs Poole is one large lady. She's twenty stone at least. And the post office doorway is one of those narrow, Victorian shop entrances.

They got stuck. He tried to force his way out, but in Mrs Poole's day it was ladies first, so she wasn't giving way. And when she realised he was covered in paint, which was now rubbing off on her neat tweed suit, she was furious. She started hitting him around the head with her handbag, which apparently contained a brick because with the first blow he went white and dropped to the floor. At least he would have dropped to the floor if he hadn't been wedged in the doorway with Mrs Poole. As it was, he slumped forward over her, his head coming to rest on her ample bosom.

I felt sorry for him then. I can think of no worse place to rest your head.

Doris or Beatrice must have pressed a panic button, because right then the police arrived. The robber was arrested, and statements were taken from each of the ladies and me.

I turned out to be a hero. Well, Sally was the hero really, but because it was me who'd brought her, the ladies were all over me. They made me tea, sat me down, and fussed over me as though I was their favourite grandson. It was all a bit much, really.

I was just about to leave when I remembered what I'd come in for. At least there'd be no problem getting my money out now.

'Six hundred?' boomed Mrs Poole. 'What on earth for? I don't know, all these young men just walk in here off the street and think they can take all our money whenever they like. Get out, lad, and take that filthy dog with you! Out, out!'

The End

Fearsome Threesome – Discussion

This story began life as an anecdote which I only half-remembered by the time I came to write the story, but which involved a post-mistress who refused to do as a burglar told her, in case it sparked off her angina. She acted the doddery old lady and managed to press the panic button. And I'd read (in *The Weekly News*!) about an unusual insurance claim – a golden retriever who'd wagged its tail in a paint tray and showered a living room in paint drips. Put the two together, add imagination and stir thoroughly, then garnish with farcical detail and you've got a story. This one, of course, is another Category 1 story. Pure silliness.

Another way to categorise stories is to decide what noise you want your readers to make when they get to the end. Yer wot? I can hear you all say. I'll explain. Obviously you don't want them to yawn, but do you want them to sniff back tears, say Ooh!, Ahh! or Ha Ha Ha! at the end?

> Ooh – twist endings. *Ooh, I didn't see that coming!*
> Ahh – sweet, thoughtful, leaves you with a smile, my category 2 and 3s
> Ha Ha Ha – the funny ones, my category 1s.
> Sniff – reaching for a tissue, the emotional ones, category 4 and 5.

As with any form of categorisation, knowing what ending noise you're aiming for can help you immensely while writing your story. Don't add Ha Ha moments if you're aiming for a Sniff ending – it'll spoil the mood and muddle the story. And vice versa – no sad bits if you want your reader to guffaw at the end.

Stewing Time

I mentioned above the components which went into *Fearsome Threesome*. But for this story, there was one more essential ingredient – time. Very often stories need time away from their authors, in which to mature. This one certainly did. I wrote it quickly, the first draft written in one evening. Then I read it back through and thought, what a load of old rubbish. I was disappointed – a good anecdote totally spoilt. Ah well, it happens. I closed the document, went to bed, and left the story alone for a couple of weeks. When I went back to it, I realised it wasn't as bad as I'd thought, and set to work knocking it into shape.

It took a few hours and a fair bit of hard work, but eventually I ended up with something I thought was worth submitting. And it was – it was bought by the first market I sent it to.

Never give up on your stories. Immediately after writing them you're just too close to be able to judge whether they're any good or not. Let them rest, and when you come back to them, you may well find they've improved with age, like a good wine.

Stewing time is also important for ideas. Sometimes if you write a story the moment you think, hey, that would make a good story, it's too soon. Your story might come out too short, or too slight, or not layered enough. The best thing to do with an idea is jot it down in a notebook, and leave it to mature. If it's a good one, you'll find yourself thinking about it, developing the idea in the back of your mind while you're doing other things such as the day job, the dishes or driving. Add thoughts to your notebook. Only sit down to write the story when you can't bear it any longer and you simply have to get it out of your head and onto the page.

I find this is a particularly important technique when writing an emotional story. If you try it too early it comes out without enough emotion. Of course if you leave it too long, you might go off the boil and lose interest, so be careful to judge this right. Writers who have to juggle day jobs, child care and other responsibilities along with writing tend to be experts at this – if an idea arrives while at work on a Monday morning, with no writing time available until the following weekend, there's no choice but to let the idea rest and mature during the week.

The next story is at the opposite end of the spectrum from the last two, and as such, needed plenty of stewing time before I wrote it. Not only that, but I decided to tell the story from a distance, to give it the perspective which comes with time. Sometimes this reduces the emotional impact of a story, but in this case I felt it was the right thing to do. See what you think.

Rosie's Legacy

I've a lot to thank her for, little Rosie, my tiny daughter who never was. She would have been about six by now. Tom thinks I'm mad to refer to her as though she was a real person, but in my mind she's real – at least she was, for a short while. I believed in her, I spent every waking hour thinking about her. And she did such a lot for me, for us, for our whole family.

If it wasn't for Rosie, I truly believe Tom and I might have separated. The boys, Ben and Alex, would have spent their weekdays with me and every second weekend with Tom. It would have messed them up emotionally, of course. They were at that sensitive adolescent stage, when a family break-up could have scarred them for life.

Thank goodness that didn't happen. Now, aged eighteen and twenty, they've grown into beautiful well-adjusted young men. We're so proud of them both. Ben moved in with his lovely girlfriend last year, and Alex is about to leave home to go to college. That's why Rosie's been in my mind lately. If she'd been here, I'd still have a child at home. As it is, by Saturday it'll be just me and Tom. It'll be wonderful, and yet, there was a time when I'd have dreaded this stage.

I was forty when it happened. Looking back, I can see we'd fallen into a rut, a downward spiral which if unchecked, would have led to the break-up of our family. We never did anything together any more. There was no time for *us*, as a family. Tom and I would leave the boys playing for hours on their Playstation or watching DVDs, while we rowed endlessly in the kitchen. I can't even remember what we argued about. Nothing of any importance – just whose turn it was to wash the saucepans, or whose fault it was that there was no bread left and no spare loaves in the freezer. The summer before we'd even taken separate holidays. The boys had spent a week with each set of grandparents, Tom had gone away with his golfing friends, and I'd stayed at home, fiddling about in the garden and going on endless shopping trips to buy clothes I didn't really need.

Then one day I realised my period was late. Not just a day or two, but a week and a half late. And I'd always been so regular.

I sweated for three days before I told Tom. Three days of praying my period would start. Three days of trying to figure out what we would do – how we could possibly cope with another baby. Our family was complete: the boys were eleven and thirteen, and we'd never wanted more than two children. We lived in a three-bedroom house – where would we put a third child? The boys would have to share, or maybe we could convert the attic. How would they cope with a baby sibling?

My career was just beginning to go somewhere. I was still working part-time but had agreed to increase my hours when Alex moved to secondary school. My employer had promised me a good pay rise and more responsibility. If I had to go back to square one with a tiny baby, at my age that would end any hopes of a proper career. I did the maths. I'd be forty-one when the baby was born, and fifty-three before the child went to secondary school. At least fifty-nine before he or she left home.

On the third day, I'd begun to think of the baby as a girl. The more I thought about it, the more I was convinced. Somehow I felt different in this pregnancy than with the boys – proof, I told myself, that I was carrying a girl. Rosie was the name 'left over' from the boys – the name we'd decided on if either of them had been a girl – and so I began thinking of her as Rosie.

It was a short step from giving her a name to seeing how she could fit into the family. I began, that day, to imagine myself buying little pink outfits for her. I could see her as a toddler, sitting on the sofa surrounded by cuddly toys. As a four-year old, dressing Barbie. As a six-year old, wearing fairy wings I would make for her. As a teenager, trailing around the fashion shops with me.

In my head, by the time I plucked up the courage to tell Tom, I was already the mother of a little girl.

Telling him wasn't easy. There'd been more and more distance between us as the years went on, and to tell the truth we hardly ever spoke any more except if absolutely necessary. Apart from the pointless arguments, of course.

I picked my moment. We'd eaten dinner, the boys were at Scouts and the six o'clock news was over. Tom was reaching for his newspaper when I told him.

'You're what? How far gone? Why didn't you tell me?'

'I'm telling you now, aren't I?' It was just like Tom to get angry straight away.

'You could have told me before you took the test, Carol. I might have wanted to be with you, while you did it.'

'Tom, I haven't taken the test yet.' Truth was, I'd been scared to. Terrified of confirming that our lives were going to be turned upside down. Terrified of seeing the proof of that little baby who was going to be born into a family on the brink of collapse.

'You haven't? So you don't know, for sure...'

'Tom, I'm two weeks late. That's never happened before.'

'Always a first time,' he muttered, before hanging his head, his elbows resting on his knees.

I stared at the back of his head. Why did he have to turn this, of all conversations, into a row? I went upstairs and threw myself onto the bed. A minute later I heard the front door slam. He'd gone out. Running away, I supposed, as I reached for a tissue.

By the time he returned, about fifteen minutes later, I'd worked myself into a state. He didn't want this baby, but I was beginning to. Rejecting the baby meant he was rejecting me, and the boys, too. How could he? If he was going to leave us, I was determined he'd have to pay full maintenance. I'd manage, somehow, to bring the boys up and look after the baby alone. I'd find a way.

'Carol?' There was a tap at the door of our bedroom.

'Go away,' I spat.

'Carol, listen, sorry about earlier. It was just the shock, that's all. I didn't mean to snap at you. Can I come in?'

Well, he did sound apologetic. He came in, clutching a paper bag from the late-night chemist's.

'A pregnancy test. We need to know, for sure. Do you want to do it now?' He handed it to me. I took the pack out of the bag and began reading the instructions. It was the same type I'd used when I had the boys – wee on a stick and wait a few minutes. If you get two blue lines you're pregnant; just one means it's a false alarm.

Tom continued talking. 'Carol, I was thinking hard while I was out. We can make this work, you know. We'll move Alex into Ben's room; it's bigger. If we get them bunk beds they'll be so excited they won't mind sharing.

Then we can decorate the little room; make a nice nursery out of it. The boys' cot is still in the attic, so's the pram, but I think we got rid of the car-seat?'

'Yes, we did,' I called from the bathroom.

Tom continued talking to me from the other side of the door. 'And money-wise we're fine if you wanted to give up work. Or if you didn't, my mum's close enough, and I'm sure she'd be happy to have the baby. She always wished she'd had more to do with the boys when they were little.'

I emerged from the bathroom holding the stick. 'We have to wait three minutes. Tom, do you really think we could manage?'

'Of course we could. You know, there's nothing like a baby for making you feel young again. And maybe it'll be a little girl. That'd complete our family, in a way. Although another boy would be easier – we'd know what we're doing.'

'I'd like a little girl. We could call her Rosie.'

'Rosie, yes, that would be lovely.'

I looked up at Tom. His eyes were glistening, and there was a tiny smile hiding at the corners of his mouth. He put out his arms to me.

'Carol, love, come here. We've been so stupid, haven't we? Always arguing, always trying to score points over each other, never stopping to look at what we have. I'm sorry. We'll start over. This baby will bring us back together, all of us.'

I put my arms round him and buried my face into his neck. It felt like coming home. 'I'm sorry, too,' I murmured.

Tom gently eased the pregnancy test out of my hand. 'Three minutes must be up.'

I let go of him and looked at the stick, then at Tom, my darling husband. Tears were pouring down both our faces.

'Oh Tom!'

'It's negative,' he said.

'There's no baby,' I said.

'No Rosie.'

'But...'

'It changes nothing, Carol. What I said – about being sorry, starting over – we can still do that.'

'We must, for the boys.'

'Yes, for our boys. And for us.'

Of course, that was only the beginning. We had a long way to go, but we'd made a start. We'd recognised we had a problem, a problem we both wanted to solve. And they say that's always the most important step, don't they?

We were both disappointed, and at the same time relieved, that there was no baby. A week later when my period finally arrived we even discussed whether we should actively try for another baby, but decided against it. Instead we worked on getting our family life and our relationship back on track.

It took time, but we succeeded. That all happened seven years ago. Now our boys are flying the nest and guess what? We're planning a second honeymoon. We're off to Venice next week. Just Tom and me and little Rosie's legacy.

The End

Rosie's Legacy – Discussion

This story was originally published in a *Take A Break* seasonal special. It's one I'm very fond of, and not just because it was a good earner. I think it's a story many women can relate to – who hasn't at some point in their life thought, oh my God, what if I'm pregnant? I rate this as a category 5 story, an emotional tear-jerker. And yet it's not a sad story, is it? There was no baby, no miscarriage, and the couple managed to mend their marriage as a result of this episode, giving us a happy ending (remember the comedy story arc?). But that scene – those three minutes while they wait for the pregnancy test results, the three minutes when little Rosie both exists and yet doesn't exist kind of like Schrödinger's cat – well, it brings a tear to my eye every time I read it. And I think it works better because the main scene is told as a flashback.

Story Structure

Story-writing advice often suggests you start the story at the moment of action. If I'd followed that advice for *Rosie's Legacy*, I'd have had to start with the pregnancy test scene. But if I had, we wouldn't have known what happened next, and why it was such a pivotal moment in the characters' lives. I think the perspective of distance: telling the story seven years on, when it's all resolved, works well in this case. The circular structure – starting in the present (Carol reflecting on her sons leaving home), long flashback, then return to the present (plans for a second honeymoon) – helps frame the main, emotional scene.

I've used this kind of circular structure in many of my short stories. While I've moved away from including flashback in my novels, I think it can work well in short stories. In this one it allowed me to show all that hinged on the main action ahead of showing that scene, so the reader knew what was at stake. I was able to begin at the end, showing there's a happy ending to come even though the first line suggests the story might involve a miscarriage. In other stories, flashback has allowed me to start at a dramatic moment, and then go back and explain how the character came to be there, and then return to the drama and its resolution. Kind of a three-act play:

1. Action scene – first part
2. Flashback – how did we come to be here
3. Action scene – second part and resolution

If you've written a story which begins too slowly and perhaps seems flat at the start, try restructuring it in a circular fashion as above. It might work better like that.

There are other structures you can try, of course, aside from linear or circular ones. Consider using a diary format, a list format, alternating viewpoints, linked sub-titles such as seasons, colours or moods, or be really brave and go backwards in time – show the ending first then the middle and then the beginning… Don't be afraid to experiment. It might not work, but if it does it'll certainly be original. Some magazines prefer straightforward, linear stories but others seem to go for the unusual formats. As always, study the markets to discover this for yourself!

The next story also plays with structure, alternating stories in two time periods. It was originally published in *My Weekly*.

The Church of Mary O'Reilly

The cleared woodland behind the half-built church was the best place Mary knew to find firewood. The workmen had taken the best timber and stacked it in a nearby barn, ready to create the roof trusses. But they'd left plenty of smaller branches lying around, part rotted but still good to burn if you dried them out. Mary picked her way carefully among the tree stumps and piles of earth dug from the church's foundations, gathering sticks which she carried in her long, tattered brown skirts.

When she'd collected enough, she made her way back across what would have become the churchyard, if it had ever been completed.

'Shame,' she muttered. 'A crying shame. Ballydunlin needs a new church, so it does. It's too far to go to St Columba's, and the old chapel is too small.'

She stopped and thought for a while. At least, the chapel *had* been too small, but these days, after the famine and emigration, the congregation was so much reduced that the chapel accommodated it easily. Work had stopped on the new church three years before when the famine first hit, and now it didn't look likely to ever resume. Who would pay for it? The English lord who'd started the project had sold his land when the Hunger carried off half his labourers. The community had no money, and no men left to finish the building. Mary's own sons were scattered – one in England, two in America and another buried alongside his father in St Columba's churchyard.

Before the famine, Mary had dreamed of seeing her children and grandchildren married in this church. But that could never happen now.

She sighed, and returned to her tiny one-roomed cottage. She built a fire in the grate, her icy fingers fumbling with the flint. In a blackened saucepan hanging over the fire she placed a single potato for her dinner. Her eyes closed for a moment as she whispered thanks to God for ending the famine and allowing the potatoes to grow unblighted once more.

'But what I don't understand, love,' said Hal, taking Leanne's hand as they left the bus stop and headed towards the church, 'is why you want us to get married in a village in the middle of Ireland. You're not even Irish!'

'I am, a little bit,' replied Leanne. 'My great-great-grandfather was Irish. He came over to England to escape the Famine, my grandmother said. He came from here, Ballydunlin. She told me the full story when I showed her my engagement ring.'

'So tell me,' Hal said.

'Wait till we get there!' laughed Leanne. 'Look, it's just around this corner.'

A yew-lined path led up to the grey-stone church, which nestled in a churchyard backed by woodland. Its spire towered above the trees, standing proudly against an azure blue sky.

'It's beautiful!' whispered Leanne. Her eyes shone as she imagined herself in a cloud of white silk, walking up this path with her father; Hal waiting inside. 'Come on, Hal. There's something I want to find.'

They pushed open the heavy wooden door. Inside was unexpectedly bright, flooded with light from several tall windows. There was colourful artwork on the walls, and a huge gilt crucifix suspended over the altar.

'Should be on this side, somewhere,' said Leanne, pulling Hal down the left-hand aisle. 'Half way down, Gran said, on the wall.'

'What are we looking for?' asked Hal.

'My ancestor,' Leanne replied.

Mary had been hunting for firewood again. The weather hadn't let up for days, and the wind still blew fiercely. But she'd run out, and knew she must collect some more or she'd freeze to death. Wrapped in several old shawls, she'd ventured out to her usual spot behind the church. There wasn't much wood left, but she'd gathered enough for one night at least, before struggling home.

Pinned to her cottage door was a letter. She frowned as she unpinned it and brought it inside. Mary couldn't remember the last time she'd received a letter. It was bound to be bad news. Perhaps she was to lose her home? Or, God forbid, maybe one of her remaining sons who had emigrated had died...

Her hands shook as she opened it. She spread it out on her table and sat down to read, carefully following the words with her finger. She thanked the Lord that her father had sent her to the priest for reading lessons when she was young.

To Mary O'Reilly, neé McGuire, the letter read. *You are required to present yourself at the offices of Sullivan and Sullivan, High Street, Ballydunlin at the earliest possible opportunity, for business concerning the late Michael McGuire, of New York City.*

Mary gasped. Michael McGuire? Her Uncle Mickey? She'd never known him, but her father had often spoken of his brother who'd gone to sea as a youth and never returned. She re-read the letter three times, then carefully tucked it into her purse.

'Here she is,' whispered Leanne. She ran her fingers over an angel adorning a beautifully carved tomb set into a niche in the church wall. 'Mary O'Reilly. My great-great-great-grandmother.'

'That's a pretty special tomb,' said Hal. 'She must have been rich?'

'No, she was very poor, Gran said. Lived in a one-room cottage, ate nothing but spuds.'

'But this tomb?'

'Two years before she died, she came into some money. A long-lost relative made a fortune but died intestate, and his solicitors tracked her down as his heiress. She kept part of the money to pay for her tomb.'

'What did she do with the rest?'

'She built this church! She spent every penny on it. So you see, it kind of belongs to our family. Gran came here to marry fifty-two years ago. And I'd like to get married here too. There's something special about it.'

Hal smiled at Leanne, and pulled her close as a shaft of sunlight suddenly illuminated the tomb. 'I think it's a great idea. And you know what? I think Mary O'Reilly approves, too.'

The End

The Church of Mary O'Reilly – Discussion

My favourite type of novels are time-slip – where two stories in different time periods alternate, inform each other and eventually come together. (For the best examples, try books by Kate Morton or Katherine Webb.) Here, I tried to use that structure in a 1000-word story. It's very tight, but I think it works.

The historical part of the story was inspired by a legend my brother-in-law told me once, about a poor woman who spent an inheritance building a church after the Irish potato famine. I needed something to relate that to the present day, and what better way than to use the church, and of course weddings are the best thing that happen in churches (in my opinion!). I liked having the family history link too. Recently I've been writing novels with a family history element, using a time-slip structure, so you might say this story was a good training ground for me.

In the first section, I needed to get across the time period (early 1850s, just after the Great Famine), the country (Ireland), and Mary's extreme poverty, all without saying something like 'Mary O'Reilly, in 1850s Ireland hadn't a penny'. The poverty was the easy one to cover – have her hunting for firewood. The nationality was pretty easy too – her name's Irish, the name of the town (fictional, but Irish-sounding), her references to God. And for the time period, I gave her long skirts at the beginning and then mentioned the famine and emigration. Of course I was relying on the reader having a little bit of historical knowledge here. I suspect if a reader was completely unaware of the devastating famine in Ireland in the 1840s-50s they might find the first part of the story confusing but even so, the end should be satisfying.

It's a tricky call, writing this kind of story. You don't

want your short story sounding like a history lesson. But you do want your readers to understand where and when the story's set, so they 'get' it. How much to put in, and how much to assume? One of the best ways to find out whether you've got it right is to try it out on readers. Get your mum, best friend or spouse to read it, and ask their opinion – did they understand the story's setting? Better still, read your story out to a writing group whose members you trust to be honest and tell you whether it works or not. Then tweak – add a bit, remove a bit – until you're sure you've got the balance right. That's what I did with *Mary O'Reilly*.

Check your facts

It's essential when writing a historical story to check your facts. Actually, you should check facts for *any* story, no matter what the time period. Nothing spoils a read more than a jarring inaccuracy (well, apart from a misplaced apostrophe, perhaps). These days, there's no excuse for getting facts wrong. Most people are online while they are writing; either typing a first draft directly onto their computer or transcribing a hand-written story and editing it as they go. And if you're online, then facts are at your fingertips. There's wonderful Wikipedia and good old Google, waiting to help. The answer you seek will be out there somewhere. So don't guess, don't assume – check!

I remember reading a story in which a girl, with some very contemporary name – Chardonnay or something – had just bought a new CD to celebrate passing her 'O' levels. Hmm. 'O' levels (UK secondary school qualifications, for the benefit of any non-UK readers) were replaced by GCSEs in 1988. The girl's name was far too modern for a teenager in the mid-eighties. CDs were introduced in 1983 but weren't really mainstream until a good few years later. Certainly a young girl in the 1980s wouldn't have been buying CDs, she'd have bought LPs or cassettes. I'm certain of this because I remember that era, but also because I've just Googled those two facts, and checked them on Wiki. When reading this story, I remember being totally confused as to when it was set. I suspect the writer meant the story to be contemporary and had simply made a mistake by referring to 'O' levels instead of GCSEs. But it spoilt the story for me.

When writing *Mary O'Reilly* I knew the dates of the Irish famine but checked them anyway. I wanted a fictional town, so came up with a place name and then Googled to check it didn't actually exist. It took seconds.

Google, dear reader, is your friend.

We were talking earlier about structure. Here's a story which starts at a dramatic moment to hook the reader, and feeds in the back story bit by bit later on, but without using flashback. Originally published in *Take A Break's Fiction Feast*.

Breaking Point

'Jemma's been suspended from school.'

It was not the sort of news I liked to be greeted with, as I struggled through the door with five bags of grocery shopping.

'Oh my God. What for?' I asked my husband Mike as I dumped the bags in the kitchen.

'She was caught shoplifting in her lunch break. She was wearing her uniform, prefect badge and all. The Head's furious. *I'm* furious, Sue.' Mike thumped the kitchen table, making the apples in the fruit bowl bounce.

I felt more resigned than furious. It was just another thing to deal with. How much more were we expected to take? It was two months since Tommy's road accident but there was no sign of him being allowed home yet. I'd been more or less living at the hospital, leaving our older children – fifteen-year old Jemma and thirteen-year old Nathan – fending for themselves at home until Mike got in from work. At least, Nathan was *supposed* to fending for himself at home, but he'd taken to running off somewhere every couple of days.

'Where is she?' I asked, as I began to put the shopping away. I wanted to get back to the hospital for the evening's visiting hours. And I needed to have words with Nathan about his disappearing acts.

'Upstairs.' Mike went through to the living room, leaving the shopping on the table.

I set off up the stairs to see her, framing a ticking-off in my head. Why did she do it? Didn't she realise how hard it was for me and her dad, with one child bashed and broken in hospital and another who keeps being brought home by friends' parents and on one occasion, the police. Didn't she realise how hard it was for *me*, having to deal with all this, as well as a husband who responded to each new crisis with anger followed by abdication?

But when I got to Jemma's room the door was closed and barricaded, and a muffled voice called out, 'Just go away Mum, all right? I'm sorry, whatever, but spare me the lecture right now. I can't face it.'

I decided I couldn't face it either, so I took a leaf out of her book, went into my own room and shut the door. I lay on the bed, face in my pillow, and sobbed. How much more? I wished time could be suspended while I dealt with one problem at a time. Better still, if time could be wound back, and I could catch hold of Tommy's arm *before* he ran across the road in front of that van...

That was when it had all started. Tommy had broken both arms, one leg, and had damaged some vertebrae. He'd had to lie flat on his back for the last two months, with his leg in traction. I'd slept in a bed beside him in the hospital for the first week. Since then, I'd been spending every moment possible at his side. I felt so helpless, but being with him was all I could do.

Nathan. I remembered I'd wanted a talk with him before going back to the hospital. Reluctantly I heaved myself off the bed and went to his room, picking up socks and underpants from the floor on the way.

He wasn't there. I headed downstairs. 'Mike, where's Nathan?'

'In his room,' Mike grunted, looking annoyed that I'd interrupted him watching the news.

'No, he's not.'

'Well he was when I came home. If that lad's run off again I'll…' I winced as the TV remote control bounced off the floor and fell apart, its batteries scattering.

'Bet that blinking thing won't work now,' Mike grumbled. 'Aren't you supposed to be back at the hospital already? And what did Jemma have to say about the suspension?'

I'm not sure what happened next. Time stopped while I completely lost control. I opened my mouth, and screamed. Simply screamed, long, loud and hard.

Jemma came charging down the stairs and stood open-mouthed, watching me. Mike stared, his mouth opening and closing like a goldfish. And still I screamed, until my throat protested and I had to stop.

For a moment the silence was intense. We all just looked at each other. Then I grabbed my purse and keys, and left the house.

Should I go to the hospital where Tommy was expecting me or go looking for Nathan?

I did neither. Instead, I got in my car and drove. Southwards, out of town, towards the coast. I parked in a cliff-top car park, got out of the car and stood, in the dark, on the cliff edge.

'Why?' I shouted into the wind. 'Why us? Why me? Why does all this have to happen to my family? How am I supposed to deal with it all?'

There was a bench nearby. I sat down, leaned back and let the wind blow my hair back from my face. If only my troubles could be blown away as easily.

'Come on, Sue,' I told myself. 'Get a grip.'

But I needed some time.

For the thousandth time I relived the moment when that anonymous white van hit Tommy and drove off. The hours which followed – frantic phone calls from hospital corridors. Stroking Tommy's face as he lay sedated under a crisp sheet. Calming Mike down, when he wanted to go searching for the white van – any white van – so he could punch the driver. Explaining what had happened to Jemma and Nathan.

I thought about the weeks since. Those endless hours at the hospital, keeping Tommy company while his bones knitted themselves back together. Rushing around at home, trying to keep on top of the housework and shopping so the rest of the family could get on with their lives.

Gradually I began to realise that in dealing with Tommy's accident I had cut out the rest of the family. When had I last talked to Jemma or Nathan apart from to shout at them or tell them off? When had I last spent time with Mike, other than passing him in the hallway as he came in from work and I headed to the hospital? And maybe his anger was simply caused by his own feelings of helplessness – feelings I knew only too well.

My family, not just Tommy, was broken, and it was up to me to mend it.

The fresh night air had worked its magic and calmed me down. A quick couple of phone calls assured me Nathan was safe and well at a friend's house, and would be dropped home later. Jemma was still sulking but Mike's anger had dissipated. I was free to go and visit Tommy.

It was a thirty minute journey to the hospital. When I arrived Tommy was sitting up with his back brace on and his broken leg stretched along the bed. His arm casts had been taken off a couple of days before, and he was enjoying being able to move a bit more and play with his Transformers.

'Mum, I had fizzy-therapy today, they made me stretch my arms like this!' Tommy stretched his arms up and out, narrowly missing knocking his glass of water from the bedside cabinet. 'I've got to practise every hour to get my muscles back.'

'Well done, darling! Soon you'll be my little Superman again. Now you've got your back brace fitted I hope you'll be able to come home soon.'

'Good. I miss home. I even miss Jemma, a bit. And Nathan, but I bet he still won't let me go on his Playstation.'

'He will. I'll make sure of that.' A vision of Tommy back home, curled in a beanbag while he played on the Playstation brought tears to my eyes. I wanted it so much.

I played with him a while, read him a story and helped get him ready to sleep. Before leaving I put away his toys and kissed him goodnight. Soon I hoped I'd be able to do that in our own home.

Back home, Mike was half way through a bottle of wine and a DVD. The kids were in their rooms. I poured myself a glass and sat down beside him.

'Tommy's on good form,' I said.

'That's great,' he replied. 'And you're not screaming.'

'Not any more,' I said, smiling. 'Sorry I lost it, earlier. It's the strain.'

Mike took my hand and squeezed it. 'I know, love. Sorry I was angry. Same excuse, I guess.'

I squeezed his hand in return. 'Better go and talk to our errant kids. Save me some wine.'

I went to Nathan's room first. He was in bed, reading his collection of Beano comics.

'Hi, Nathan,' I said. 'I hear you were at Jake's this evening. Did you have a good time?'

'Yeah, s'pose,' he said, looking at me defensively.

'Nathan, look. It's fine for you to go to your friends' houses. Just tell us where you are, please.'

'You're never here to tell.'

'I know. I'm sorry. But you could leave a note. Or text. So we know, and we don't worry. Deal?'

He looked stunned that I hadn't shouted at him, like I had the last few times he'd pulled this stunt.

'Deal?' I asked again.

He smiled – that lopsided shy smile which never failed to tug at my heartstrings. 'Deal, Mum.'

We shook on it, and I went to tackle Jemma next. She was draped face down across her bed, her eyes smudged black with mascara and dried tears. I suspected she'd been there all evening.

'Tell me,' I asked quietly, perching on her homework desk, 'what happened.'

To my astonishment my tough teenage daughter climbed off her bed and flung her arms around my neck, sobbing.

'It was a transformer. That Optimus Prime one Tommy's always wanted. It was the last one on the shelf and I didn't have the money. I'd have gone back tomorrow to pay for it, I would have, really.'

'You stole it for Tommy?'

'I miss him, Mum. I wanted to send him something to play with now he's got his arms back. I tried to explain to the security guard but he wouldn't listen. Neither would the Headmistress.'

'I'll phone her tomorrow. I understand why you did it but, Jemma…'

'I know. I won't do it again.' She grabbed a handful of tissues from her box and blew her nose loudly. 'I thought you'd shout at me, Mum.'

I hugged her tight. I'd clearly been doing far too much shouting lately.

The phone rang, calling me back downstairs. It was the hospital, making an appointment for me to meet with Tommy's doctor the next morning. When I heard what he wanted to discuss, I found myself grinning broadly.

'Jemma, Nathan, come downstairs for a minute,' I called.

Mike looked up in surprise as we all traipsed into the living room. The kids looked terrified. Perhaps they thought their parents were playing good cop, bad cop.

'Pause the DVD,' I said to Mike. 'I've got something to say.'

Mike pressed a button on the remote. 'Go on.'

'I'm meeting Dr Millbank tomorrow. To discuss when Tommy can come home.'

Nathan whooped, Jemma squealed, but my eyes were on Mike. His face broke gradually into a wide grin. 'Sue, that's fantastic!' He raised his glass and clinked mine. As he enfolded me in a bear-hug, I realised it wasn't just Tommy's broken bones that were finally healing. Our family life had fallen apart for a while but with Tommy home we'd be able to get back on track. We'd pull through, all of us together, I was sure of it.

The End

Breaking Point – Discussion

This is another category 5 story, and hopefully you found it emotional too. Poor little Tommy, and poor old Sue too, having so much thrown at her. I wrote this story in response to a prompt from an online writing group I belonged to – the prompt was to write about a dysfunctional family which becomes functional again.

As you've seen it starts at a dramatic moment, when Sue is told her daughter's been suspended from school for shop-lifting. This, together with Nathan's disappearance, Tommy's hospitalisation and Mike's unhelpful grumpiness tips her over the edge (and indeed, *Take A Break* published it under the title *Mum on the Edge*. Many magazines change titles when they buy stories. Although the editors say a great title helps catch their eye, don't fret if you can't think of one. If an editor likes the story they'll buy it regardless of its title.)

The back story – Tommy's accident and the events afterwards, are fed in bit by bit as the story unfolds. If you've got a lot of back story to tell, and you don't want to include it as a scene in flashback, make sure you don't dump it all on the reader in one hit, as this can slow the pace. Drip-feed it in. If you look at the first half of *Breaking Point,* you'll see the first mention of Tommy's accident comes in paragraph 5, then there's a bit more in paragraph 8, then in paragraphs 10 and 11 we hear more detail of what happened. But it's not till half way through, when Sue is screaming into the wind on the cliff top (I like that image – it's powerful and conveys her frustration and helplessness) that we get to relive the accident with Sue. I could have used flashback here but decided I wanted the reader to stay with Sue, in the present, on the cliff top. There are always many ways in which you can progress your story, and it might take you a couple of attempts until you find the best way, to create the effect you want.

You might also find you need to 'write your way in'. If you're not sure where to start the story, just start writing anyway. Once you've reached the end, the beginning may be clearer, and you can simply cut the waffly start in the editing process.

Editing

So let's talk a little about editing. For many writers, this is where the fun begins. I have heard of several who say first drafts are brought into the world kicking and screaming, dragged out unwillingly; whereas the refining, tightening and honing of the editing process is the part they enjoy and the part where the story really takes shape. I wouldn't go as far as that. When the writing's flowing I love, *really* love, creating the first draft. But I do also enjoy knocking a messy mound of words into shape – it is extremely satisfying to re-read after a tough editing session and know the story is far, far better than before.

Most stories need several passes through at the edit stage. Some come out almost perfect, but that's rare. (At least, it's rare for me.) I try to look at different problems during each edit, for example:

1. Structural and plot problems. Did I start in the right place? Does the plot hang together? Did my characters manage to keep the same name throughout the story?

2. Once the structure and plot are ok, I'll look at the characterisation, dialogue, setting. Have I unfolded

my characters properly? Is the dialogue realistic? Do I need a touch more or less description?

3. Now it's beginning to look reasonable. I'll then move on to sentence flow – does it read smoothly, or are there run-on sentences or awkward sentence constructions?

4. Finally, but not always, I'll read the story aloud. Your eye tends to skip over difficult bits, and you read what you think should be there rather than what is actually written. But when you read it aloud you're using a different part of your brain, and you're forced to read every word. You'll undoubtedly spot more errors this way, even though you thought it was perfect before. Edit by ear.

5. During all editing stages I'll correct typos and punctuation mistakes as soon as I spot them. Actually I usually correct them as I'm typing the first draft, if I notice them then. (Years of being a computer programmer have made me quick to notice small errors in text. One misplaced full stop in a computer program and the darned thing won't compile. And it won't even tell you exactly where the error is.)

I find editing needs a different mindset from that of first-draft writing. It's not as creative, or at least it's a different type of creativity. There's less freedom. The world's no longer your oyster because your story already has a start, a middle and an end, characters, setting, a point to make. You've made choices and most of them you'll need to stick with, unless you want to start again and write a whole different story. You've written all the right words, but they're not necessarily in the right order. You may need to be ruthless while editing and cut out whole chunks – keep a clear, dispassionate head and do what needs to be done. And don't forget to leave a gap of a week or two between writing the first draft and editing so that you come back to it with fresh eyes.

There's quite a lot going on in *Breaking Point*. It could almost be expanded into a novel. Actually, with the addition of sub-plots, and sections told from different points of view, it *could* be a novel. That's not true of most short stories, and certainly not true of the next one, which is a very short 'moment in time' story, first published in *My Weekly*.

Queen of the Dawn

If I'm really careful, I can avoid the creaky stairs. They come with the territory in three-hundred year old country cottages. Fourth one down, third after that and second up from the bottom. Bottom step is ok as long as you tread on the left hand side. Cling to the banister to steady myself as I take that extra stretch down two stairs.

I tiptoe my way carefully through the jumble of Lego which adorns the tiled hallway floor. Soon I'm safely on the doormat, and undetected as yet.

I take my coat from the peg, put my gloves on, pull my hat tightly over my ears, lace my boots. Pick up keys, quietly now, slip them into my pocket. Open the door – very slowly, then it doesn't squeak. Slip out and pull it closed: there's the tiniest click as it latches. They won't have heard that.

At least I hope not. I peeped in on each, on my way past their bedrooms, and they were still sound asleep. Duvets askew, arms flung over heads, teddy bears long since knocked to the floor. My husband was still comfortably snoring as I eased myself out of his embrace – he's on the late shift this week and won't surface till lunchtime.

But I'm a morning person. And the very early morning is me-time.

I turn left out of our garden gate, and walk up the lane, past the copse of oaks, still bare but in bud, silhouetted against the grey pre-dawn.

There's a glimmer of light in the eastern sky. I head towards it, over the stile and across the fields. It's peaceful but not silent out here – the sound of birdsong fills the air. A rabbit hops away at my approach, disappearing into a burrow at the edge of the field. Behind me, Venus still shines brightly as the last outpost of Night, but its time is almost up and it is beginning to fade.

Soon I'm enveloped by a pink glow - warm like the duvet I've so recently left. But unlike in my bedroom the air here is fresh cold and invigorating, smelling of frosted earth.

At the top of the hill I pause and look towards the lightening sky. The birds are quiet now, awed by the majesty of the morning. I stand for a moment in complete silence, in absolute solitude. The first arc of the sun slips above the horizon and lights my face, crowns me Queen of the Dawn. I breathe deeply and smile. This is my world.

For a moment, anyway.

I watch, entranced as always, until the full splendour of the sun is above the horizon, and its warmth begins to melt the frost. Then I turn to leave, retracing my steps down the hill, past the copse, back into our lane. I duck under the overhanging branches of our magnolia tree, which is just days away from bursting into life with milky-white blossom. I let myself in to the house quietly, remove my boots and pad sock-clad to the kitchen – buying myself time to make a cup of tea.

But today my luck runs out early.

The kettle has only just boiled when half a dozen feet pound down the stairs, hitting all the creaky ones. Kicked Lego pieces scatter and clatter across the hallway floor. The kitchen door crashes open. I wince as it bounces back against the fridge.

The children charge in, half-dressed but fully awake, faces shining with the exhilaration of youth, the early morning of their lives.

'Mummy! Can I have an egg? Brown Bear wants one too.'

'Morning Mum. Where's breakfast? Is my football kit clean? Did you sign my homework diary?'

'Coco pops, please! Kiss kiss, Mummy.'

I laugh and kiss my three beautiful children, and set to work meeting their breakfast needs. No more solitude for this mother for a while. But I've had my moment, started my day at peace, with my feet on the earth and my thoughts in the heavens. I smile at the kids. They are my world.

The End

Queen of the Dawn – Discussion

First let me make it absolutely clear that this story is not written from life. Nothing, but *nothing* entices me out of bed before I really have to. Just shows the power of a writer's imagination!

This story began life as a flash fiction piece, written to a prompt 'solitude' and with a time limit of just 20 minutes or so. (If you're intrigued by the idea of writing like that, take a look at www.write-invite.com which runs weekly online competitions, speed-writing using prompts.) In such a short time you're unlikely to write a complete, saleable story but you might well find you've written something that can be expanded. That happened here – the first piece was just 300 words and ended with the main character standing on the hill watching the dawn. To make it into a womag story I needed to increase the length and turn it into something readers could relate to – and I think all mothers will identify with that feeling of needing a few moments to themselves at some point during the day.

So even a very short, coffee break story such as this one can contain a message or a universal truth. This one, I would say, is a category 3 story, which brings a smile of recognition to your face at the end.

When I first expanded this story and sent it off, it was set in autumn, with golden leaves littering the lane and frozen stubble in the fields. Although I submitted it in summer by the time the editor emailed me to accept it, it was the depths of winter, so she asked me to change the season to spring. Actually, I think it works better as a spring story – new life, buds bursting forth on trees like the growing kids: all that potential. I was more than happy to change it. If ever you're asked to amend a story by an editor, don't be precious about it, do what you're asked and you should make the sale. Your stories are your commodity, the editor is the customer, and is the person you need to please. Stories are bespoke, not mass-produced.

Time to Write

This looks like a good point at which to discuss that problem all writers have – lack of time. I've never yet met a writer who says, oh yes, I have more than enough time to get my writing done. Instead, the more time to write a writer has, the more ideas come, and so the bucket is always overflowing. Most writers need to fit their writing around other demands such as a day job, child care, house-keeping, elderly parent care, not to mention hobbies, fitness regimes and other interests. I'm just the same – I have a full time job (but very luckily, one I can do from home), two teenagers, a disabled mother and a husband all of whom deserve at least some of my time. I also enjoy running, Zumba, cycling and swimming, and believe that money saved is money that should be spent on holidays. It's a lot to fit in. Where can the time come from for writing?

I should hand over to my husband here, because most of the following wisdom comes from him. But although he's an inspirational amateur life coach, he's a lousy writer, so I'll paraphrase him.

- *Never* say you have no time. You have the same amount of time as everyone else, ie 24 hours a day, 7 days a week. It's how you *choose to fill your time* that varies.

- If writing is the most important thing for you, let your first thought on waking be: *when* am I going to do my writing today? Make all your other commitments fit around your writing.

- Find suitable writing-time slots in the week. Stick to them. Make sure you use those slots for actual writing, not faffing on Facebook or twiddling on Twitter.

- When you're not actually writing, you can still be thinking about writing. In fact, many of your best ideas will probably come when you are miles from your PC and doing something entirely different. Note these ideas down, so when you DO get some proper writing time, you can hit the ground running.

- Watch less TV, get up 20 minutes earlier, give up

ironing. An hour less TV can be an hour more writing time. 20 minutes a day is over two hours a week, which could be 2000 words, which could be a story a week. And ironing is a completely pointless activity anyway.

Finding Inspiration

What if you do have some time to write, and you're sitting down with a clear hour or so ahead, but then nothing comes? You have no inspiration at all. What then? Some people would call this writers' block. Well, there are ways of getting over it, and ways of avoiding it in the first place. Here are some of mine.

Avoid writers' block by:

- Knowing what you want to write before you sit down. During all those non-writing hours, while driving, washing up, bathing the kids etc, let ideas tumble around your head, and allow first lines to form. Jot those ideas down as soon as possible, so that when you come to your proper writing time you can pick the loudest one and get started immediately.

- Leave a work-in-progress in the middle of a scene, or even in the middle of a sentence. Don't shut down your computer, and don't even close the document (but do save it and back it up), so that when you return to it you can just carry on typing from where you were. This tip is especially good if you are writing longer fiction. Never leave a novel at the end of a chapter or scene – it's almost impossible to start the next one from cold. Much better to stop somewhere which is not a natural break. You'll be itching to get back to it, and when you do, you'll be able to carry on as if you've had no break at all.

- Have more than one writing project on the go, at different points in their evolution. If you feel stuck on one story, work on another. So if a new story idea seems to be going nowhere, have other stories which are awaiting editing. If you're feeling particularly non-creative one day you might find editing is just the thing – it uses a different set of skills and a different part of your brain.

And if it's too late and you've hit a block, try the following:

- Try a writing exercise. Find a prompt word (open a book and stick in a pin at random), set a kitchen timer to 6 minutes, and see if you can come up with some first lines using that prompt word. Or try to write a limerick: There once was a very blocked writer…

- Pick a character from your work-in-progress, or decide on a new character for a new story. Write a monologue in first-person from that character's point of view. This need not be anything to do with your story, just use it as a warm-up to get you going.

- Open a new computer document, switch off your monitor (or put a sheet of paper over the screen if using a laptop) and write blind. Write anything – if nothing comes to mind write about how stupid this writing exercise actually is, and why on earth you bought this book which advises you to do such ridiculous things. In fact, writing a rant about anything which annoys you can be a good way of limbering up your writing muscles.

- Don't write. Get up, close your laptop, and go out for a walk, rain or shine. Or if babysitting duties prevent this, try doing some housework or a jigsaw instead. (Or even do the ironing, but only as the very last resort!) While you're otherwise occupied, let the back of your brain come up with some new ideas.

I don't believe anyone is ever so blocked that they can't write anything at all. You may not feel you can write anything publishable but don't worry about that. Just write something, anything, and treat it as a warm-up. No athlete wins races every day, and no athlete wins a race from cold. Athletes need to train, and warm up their muscles. So do writers. When blocked, do warm-up exercises and call it a training day. You might not create anything saleable today but you'll be improving your overall writing strength for the future.

Time for another story. This one grew from an anecdote I heard somewhere. I have a soft spot for it, as it is the first one I ever sold to *Take A Break's Fiction Feast*, which later became my best market. I still recall the delight I felt on hearing of this story's acceptance. Bought myself a lovely handbag with the payment. (*Always* spend your first earnings on something special, for yourself. So that you can point at it and say, my writing paid for that!)

The Missing Piece

Clive wandered aimlessly through the store. He'd been to the book department, but what was the point, he'd never been a big one for reading. That had been Marge's territory. Always had her nose in a book or magazine, Marge had. Oh, if Clive had a penny for every time they'd been late to go out, or late to bed because he'd not been able to tear Marge away from her books…

He moved on to the Audio and TV department. No, nothing here for him either. He had a perfectly good TV in the sitting room and a radio in the kitchen. What more could he need? Dutifully he stood and stared at the displays of DVD players and digital radios. His daughter Clare had insisted he go out shopping, so he felt obliged to visit all the departments she'd listed.

'Get yourself something to cheer yourself up,' she'd told him. 'Something to keep yourself entertained in the evenings, now you're on your own.' Clive sighed. Marge had been all the entertainment he'd ever needed. He'd always been happy just to sit and look at her, watching the little movements of her eyes and her changing expressions as she read one of her books. Or observing the busy flickering of her hands as she knitted. He would let his eyes roam slowly over her profile, her strong jaw line, the little button nose that she hated and he loved, the graceful swoop of her forehead, her thick grey hair, caught at the neck in a black velvet ribbon.

Sometimes Marge would look up, aware she was being watched. She'd smile at him, that slow sensual smile which lit up her whole face. 'Stop it, love. How can I read when you're looking at me like that?'

'I can't help it, my beauty,' he'd say. And Marge would look down again at her book or knitting but her smile would remain.

Like two pieces of a jigsaw we are, Clive had often thought. We just fit perfectly together.

But now Marge was gone and Clive felt as though half of him was missing. For months now he'd spent his evenings just staring at the chair where Marge had sat. Clare was a good daughter and had spent many evenings with him chatting about this and that, putting on the TV for programs she thought might interest him. But Clare had a husband and lots of friends and couldn't spend every evening with her old dad. So she'd suggested he go shopping to look for some other way to spend his evenings.

Clive left the Audio and TV department and moved on through the shop. He passed a display of cameras. If only he'd had a camera, he'd have photos of Marge to look at now. But he'd never seen the need while she was alive. Why would he want to look at a picture of her when he had the real living beauty in front of him, he used to say. Now he regretted his earlier attitude. Already sometimes he found he couldn't quite recall the precise curve of her cheekbone, or the exact way the firelight would reflect in her eyes when she looked up at him on those evenings which now seemed so long ago.

Beyond the cameras were phones, then giftware. Finally Clive found himself looking at a fixture full of games – traditional chess, draughts and Monopoly; newer games based on TV shows; games with intriguing titles such as Mid Life Crisis, Cut and Run, Cranium. He picked up a couple and turned them over to read the description on the back of the box. For two players. Two to six players. Four or more players. No good for just him, then.

'Can I help you sir?' asked a shop assistant. Clive turned. She was young, probably still in her teens. She had friendly eyes and hair caught in a black velvet ribbon like Marge used to wear. Clive liked her at once.

'Well you see, I'm looking for something to keep me entertained in the evenings. I'm on my own, see, and my daughter thinks I need something to keep my mind occupied.'

'OK sir, let's think. Most of these games need more than one player. What about Sudoku? We've a wide range of puzzle books.'

Clive looked confused but the girl was quick to explain. 'They're logic puzzles. You have to fit numbers into a grid…'

Clive shook his head and held up a hand to stop her. He'd never been one for logic.

'No? OK, perhaps a model kit?' The sales assistant led him over to boxes which contained 'all you need to make your very own Big Ben in matchsticks'.

Clive laughed. 'I used to do things like this when I was a lad. Always building something, that was me. Oh you should have seen some of the things I made out of bits of balsa wood or Meccano. But not now, love. I just don't think my hands are steady enough for that kind of work any more. Shame, I would have enjoyed that one,' he said, pointing to a build-it-yourself model of the Eiffel Tower. He and Marge had spent a wonderful holiday in Paris five years ago. If only he had photos from that trip.

He could remember it all so clearly, walking over Pont Neuf onto the Île de la Cité. They'd walked right to the end, to the little gardens on the tip of the island where you can look along the river Seine towards the Eiffel Tower on the left and the Louvre on the right. They'd found a wrought-iron bench, and sat there until the sun went down. Clive smiled, remembering how a young photographer had asked their permission to take a photo of them. Well, they weren't to be the main subject of the photo, the lad explained, it was a general shot of the river and sunset he wanted, but with the bench and the old couple in the foreground to add interest. Marge had protested at being called 'old' and the young man had blushed, embarrassed. But Marge was only teasing and said she was only too delighted to be in his photo. Clive could still recall the way her eyes shone in the light of the setting sun as she arranged herself, leaning back against Clive's arm as the photographer directed.

'Sir? Perhaps you'd like to look at the jigsaws? If you enjoy building things you might like the challenge of these 1000-piece puzzles?'

'Now there's an idea,' Clive said. Yes, he could imagine spending time on a jigsaw. They could be quite absorbing, and satisfying when you finally completed one. And he was sure Clare would approve.

'We have some lovely scenes here; one of a steam train, another of the London skyline at dusk. Actually that's part of a series – Cities at Sunset. This one's Edinburgh, see the castle. A lot of sky to do on that one though. And here's Paris…'

Clive took the Paris puzzle from her. It was a beautiful photo, of the river Seine bathed in the pink light of the dying sun. The city skyline stood out against the sunset, and to balance it, in the bottom left the photographer had included part of the riverbank and a bench with two figures seated close together.

'Oh my word,' Clive exclaimed quietly, looking closely

at the picture. 'Oh my goodness me.'

'Is anything wrong, sir?' asked the sales assistant.

'No, no, not at all,' replied Clive, smiling. 'In fact, I think I'll take this one. It's perfect. Thank you for all your help. Just one more thing, what size will this be when it's complete? You see, I think I'd like to buy a frame to put it in when it's done. I know just the place to hang it, so I can look at it every day. What a beauty. What a beauty she is.'

The End

The Missing Piece – Discussion

I rate this as a category 3 – brings a smile and perhaps made you say Aw! at the end. One thing you'll have noticed – the main character is male. As I said at the start of this book, it is OK to use male main characters, and although the majority of the stories will have female MCs, there are always a fair few featuring men. So if a man makes the best central character for your story, use him. (And if you *are* a man, don't worry, that does not exclude you from writing for women's magazines. Plenty of men do. Some use female pseudonyms but others write under their own names. Editors certainly won't hold your sex against you, if you can write a good story. The magazines are mostly bought by women, therefore the short story market tends to be dominated by women, but don't let that put you off!)

One mistake beginner womag writers make is to assume that because the readership for a particular magazine is middle-aged to elderly, then all the characters should be in that age group too. This is not the case, and some editors are constantly crying out for more stories featuring young families. Reading short stories is a form of escapism. A widowed reader of advanced years is unlikely to want to read about a widowed character of advanced years (although there's always an exception if the editor likes the story, like my Clive in *The Missing Piece*). The reader wants to escape from their own life for a few minutes, so give them younger characters, an unusual setting, a different kind of life. As long as there's something in the story a reader can relate to.

Rules of Writing

Are there any? Beyond the obvious and important rules of spelling and grammar, I mean. If you read enough writing books and blogs and frequent enough online writing forums, you'll probably hear lots of rules being bandied about without much explanation behind them. I'm not a believer in rules. Some of the silliest I've heard are:

- Avoid using adverbs. This usually means adverbs of manner, ie the ones ending with 'ly' such as quickly, effectively, usually. Oh, oops, I've just used one (usually) when explaining what the rule meant. But words like only, often, again, very, soon, still, yesterday are also adverbs. Avoiding such words completely can lead to very convoluted language. (Just think: how could I have said that last sentence without the word 'completely'?) I would suggest: use adverbs by all means but make sure you use them *well* (as for any other word).

- Avoid using the word 'that'. Well, it is possible that sentences containing the word 'that' can be made snappier by removing it. In fact, that last sentence could have been written without 'that' as the 5th word; and this one could have used 'the' in place of 'that' as the 3rd word. But in both cases, I think including 'that' makes them more readable. It's a question of style.

- Avoid starting sentences with And or But. If you're around my age and were brought up in the UK (and perhaps had the formidable Mrs Winsey as your English teacher) you probably break out in a cold sweat every time you see a sentence beginning with and or but. It took me twenty years to throw off that rule. These days, it's perfectly acceptable. And I rather like sentences beginning with these words.

- Show, don't tell. This one gets trotted out probably more than any other. It's usually taken to mean that everything should be written as a scene, and nothing should be simply stated. Tosh. Stories generally need some parts told and some parts shown. It's all about balance. Some bits you want to skip through to get to the meat of the story, other sections you want to linger over. *Rosie's Legacy* had a long section of 'tell' at the start, until we got to the pregnancy test scene which is all 'show'. I've already explained my reasons for writing that story in this way. I think you need both tell and show in a story – the trick is in using the right technique at the right point.

There are guidelines for writing which are generally better than the stated rules. For instance:

- Start at a dramatic moment (we've already discussed this one).
- Avoid clichés – they're lazy.
- Include dialogue because it helps with pace.
- Don't go overboard with too much flowery description.
- Keep the number of named characters in a short story to four or fewer.
- Make your characters' names distinct from each other.

But all rules and guidelines can be broken. Read them, think about them, and when you fully understand them and know what you're doing, try breaking them. As I did with glee in this next story, originally published in *Take A Break's Fiction Feast*.

I Don't Know Who To Pick

Jamie's my best buddy and I love him to bits, but sometimes he can be, well, a bit slow on the uptake. The obvious solution to a problem can be staring him in the face, practically biting his nose off, and Jamie'll be completely oblivious to it. You have to point it out with flashing neon arrows and explain it in words picked from a junior dictionary, before he'll see it.

Take his wedding dilemma, for example. Who to pick as best man.

'Cheryl,' he moaned to me, as we sat clutching our mugs during coffee break. 'I just don't know who to choose. There's Matt who I've known since we were five, or Mark from the football team, or Merv from the pub.'

I laughed. 'Do all your mates have names beginning with M? Makes it very hard for me to remember who's who.'

Jamie didn't appear to hear me. 'Or I could pick Stu who I used to work with, Simon my fiancée's brother, or my own brother Steve.'

'Well it's obvious then, isn't it?' I said. 'Pick Steve, or he might feel slighted.'

Jamie groaned. 'Steve lives in Australia, his wife's expecting a baby, and he emailed me yesterday to say he'll do his best but can't promise to be at the wedding.'

'So not a good choice, then.'

'No, though if he does make it, I'd like him to play a part…'

'He could always be an usher.'

'I suppose so.' Jamie's face was longer than a rainy Sunday afternoon and just as miserable.

'Who does Sarah want you to pick?'

Jamie shrugged. 'I think she'd quite like me to pick her brother, but she said it's up to me. She chose the bridesmaids, I choose the best man. She's got two stunning little sisters, so it was an easy choice for her.'

'Do you get on well with her brother?'

'Yes, but… I think I should choose someone who's known me longer. Like Rick, maybe, or Rahul.'

I sighed. 'Who are *they*?'

'The lads from the squash club. I've known them since I joined, eight years ago.'

I drained my coffee cup and got up to go back to work. 'Well Jamie, you're going to have to make a decision soon. The wedding's in four weeks, isn't it?'

'Four weeks! God, Cheryl, you're right. Arrghh!'

I left him to his pondering.

At lunch time, Jamie and I took our sandwiches to the park as usual, and sat down on our favourite bench overlooking the duck pond. We'd been spending lunch times together since we'd joined the company as trainees, fresh from college, ten years ago. There'd never been anything romantic between us, we were just good friends. I'd been married to Ian for three years and Jamie had been with my old school friend Sarah since they met at our wedding.

'Well?' I asked him, as he popped open a can of diet Coke. 'Come to any conclusions yet?'

'Nope. I was thinking Stu, but then remembered

Matt…'

I shook my head. All those names were giving me a headache.

And then I had an idea.

'Jamie?'

'Cheryl?'

'What about….'

'Go on…'

'Well it's kind of flouting convention but…'

'I'm listening.'

'Why not… have all of them?'

Jamie choked on his Coke. 'All of them?'

'All of them.'

'What, Matt and Mark and Merv and Stu and Steve and Simon and Rick and Rahul?'

'Yep. The whole bally lot of them.'

'But that's… seven!'

'Um, eight, I make it.' This wedding business was clearly addling Jamie's head.

'Eight! I can't have eight best men!'

'Why not?'

'Because… well, people don't! They choose one.'

'So choose one.'

'I can't.'

'So have all eight.'

'Hmm.' Jamie munched on a sandwich, lost in thought.

You're a genius, Cheryl, I thought, though I say it myself. Sheer genius. I could see it now, the line of handsome men in matching suits at the altar, passing the ring along the line until it finally reached Jamie. Eight speeches. Endless toasts. Unusual, but brilliant.

And with eight best men to organise it, the stag night was likely to be unforgettable.

'Hmm,' muttered Jamie again, as he gazed at the ducks. 'You know, it might just work.' He smiled to himself, and took another bite of his sandwich.

'Glad to have helped,' I said.

'What? Oh, you have, you have. Thanks Cheryl,' he said, through a mouthful.

It was Thursday, and after work on Thursday we always went to the Red Lion to meet up with Ian and Sarah. The four of us would have a meal and a few drinks before going home. Today Ian was already there, and Sarah walked in as Jamie was waiting to be served at the bar. We found a table for four by the window.

Jamie arrived back from the bar with a bottle of champagne and four glasses.

'What're we celebrating, love?' asked Sarah.

'Me having flouted convention and made a decision about the best man,' said Jamie. 'At least I hope we can celebrate.'

'You've yet to ask them, haven't you?' I said. Suddenly I felt horribly responsible. What if some of them said no, or couldn't make it, or Sarah thought it was a terrible idea? It'd all be my fault for suggesting it.

'You're right, I haven't asked them yet. I'll do it now.' Jamie pulled out his phone, and tapped in a number.

I was sweating. Now I was going to have to listen to eight conversations, each time wondering whether it'd be a yes or a no.

Right then, my own phone rang. I pulled it out, made an apologetic face and moved away from the table to answer it. Thank goodness – it would spare me the embarrassment of eavesdropping through all those calls.

'Hello?'

'Cheryl?'

'Yes?'

'Would you do me the honour of being the best man, that is, the best *woman*, at my wedding? Because, Cheryl, *you* are my best mate.'

I hung up, went back to the table and gave Jamie an enormous hug and a sloppy kiss while Ian and Sarah whooped and cheered.

'Of course I will, you idiot!' I said. 'Took you long enough!'

We poured the champagne and clinked glasses. Like I said, sometimes it takes Jamie ages to see it, but this time the solution was right in front of him all along.

The End

I Don't Know Who To Pick – Discussion

What was that guideline about having no more than four named characters in a short story? This story is 1000 words and yet I racked up twelve names (the two main characters, their partners, and the eight potential best men).

Another good guideline when naming your characters is to avoid having names beginning with the same letter. So don't have a Matt, a Mark and a Merv all in the same story, or you'll confuse your reader.

In this one, of course, I deliberately flouted that guideline (what a rebel, eh?). It was natural for Jamie and Cheryl to use Jamie's friends' names when discussing who should be best man, so I deliberately grouped them and used the same first letters, and had Cheryl notice that, as a way of saying to the reader: don't worry too much about these characters, just take on board that there are a lot of them. I think it works. Well, I sold the story, anyway.

This is a category two story – light humour. It was inspired by a true story about a couple in Australia who had eight best men. And a girlfriend of mine was best woman at a wedding, so I combined the two ideas into one. It's a twist ending – hopefully you did not expect that Jamie had made up his mind in favour of asking Cheryl until the very end.

Twist endings

Which brings me neatly on to discuss a very common form of story found in some of the women's magazines. If you can write a good, *original* twist ending story you will almost certainly be able to sell it. But they are so darned hard to write! At least I think so.

The main twists have all been done so many times you need to come up with something really special – but it *is* possible. The trick is to make sure your story stands up well even without the twist.

If it's a good story in its own right, adding a twist ending might lift it up a notch and help you sell it. If the story doesn't really work without the twist, you probably won't sell it. So make sure you have enough layers, emotion, a good setting, rounded characters, great dialogue and that your story makes your reader think or laugh or say 'aw' and *then* add the twist.

Common twists are:

- Gender. The reader thinks the main character is a woman but at the end you reveal it is a man (or vice versa). Easiest to do if you use first person point of view (to avoid using he or she). Shamelessly exploit stereotypes – I remember one by Della Galton which opens with the main character ironing, so of course you assume it's a woman.

- Generation. The reader thinks the main character is the daughter interacting with her mother or father but actually she's the mother (or similar). For instance a woman getting ready for her wedding – we'd assume the daughter is the one getting married.

- Not human. The reader thinks the main character is a person but actually it's a dog or cat or possum or inanimate object. Don't do this one. You won't sell it.

- Occupation. The reader thinks the main character is of one occupation but actually they're not, eg the burglar is actually a cop, the murderer is actually an actor, the nervous person rushing to an interview is the boss not the job-seeker.

- Dead. The reader thinks the main character is alive but actually it's a ghost. Tricky to sell this one too – will definitely need plenty of layers to make the story work on its own.

Those are all identity twists – where the reader is misled into thinking the main character is something he or she is not. There are also situation twists, where the main character is being misled along with the reader, for instance:

- Woman sees her partner with another woman and thinks he's having an affair, but actually it's his sister.

- Main character suspects another character of something (affair, crime etc) but actually they're arranging a surprise party or holiday for the MC.

- Main character thinks boss hates her because he's giving her so much work, but actually he's preparing her for promotion.

I Don't Know Who To Pick is a situation twist. Cheryl thinks Jamie is going to start phoning all his mates but actually he's decided to ask her. But check out that last line – did she plan this all along? Did she always want to be his best woman but didn't want to suggest it outright? I like to think so.

Whereas identity twists of every type have been done very many times making it hard to find a new way of using them, there are always new situation twists.

The examples above might have been done many times but if you brainstorm a bit, you'll probably come up with a new twist. In a memorable writing class session, we did just that. Starting with the 'she thinks he's having an affair' scenario we came up with about ten alternative twist endings, none of which were the old chestnut 'but it was his sister'. In fact, one alternative I came up with I think could be a winner – must write the story soon!

Time for the next story. Here's one I sold to *The Weekly News*.

The Bet

With a week to go before he found out whether what he had done would pay off, Clive began to feel nervous. Maybe it was his imagination, but those two fellas in their black jeans and hooded tops had been walking ten paces behind him for some way now. Clive was used to people catching him up and passing him, but the two young lads seemed to be making a point of staying the same distance behind him. He would have speeded up if he could, but it was hard enough already managing both his walking frame and a bag of shopping.

Finally he reached the block where he lived, and for a moment debated going straight to the warden, rather than to his own ground floor flat. But he stopped himself.

'What would they want with a feeble old man like yourself,' he muttered. 'You're being daft, old boy. If they really were after me they could have duffed me over while I crossed the park, when there was no one to see.'

Still, as his arthritic hands fumbled with the key in the lock, Clive felt his heart pounding as the two young men approached. Maybe they'd been sent from Willis's? He cursed as he dropped the keys, then turned to face his attackers.

'I've no money,' he began. But the lads stopped in front of him, then one of them stooped to pick up his keys.

'Here y'are, mate,' he said, handing them back. Clive mumbled his thanks, and chastised himself for judging them by the way they dressed. Really, he was becoming far too paranoid, imagining Willis's might send thugs to finish him off.

Later, Clive's granddaughter Mia visited, bringing her children and a stew she'd made for his dinner.

'Hey Granddad, only a week to go, now! How are you?'

'Fine, love, thank you. What a marvellous stew! And how are my little treasures?' he said, catching his nearest great-grandchild, and pulling the giggling girl into his arms.

'They're on good form today, Granddad. They've had a busy day at the nursery – finger painting all day from what I could gather. I'll put this in the oven for you now, shall I? It'll need thirty minutes to heat through.'

'Thanks, love. You're so good to your old Granddad, Mia. Now then, you're coming to my little party next week, aren't you?'

'Of course! And are you sure you don't want me and Steve to chip in? It'll cost you a fortune, hiring that hall and paying the caterers. We don't mind, honestly.'

'I'll not hear of it, Mia. The money won't be a problem, I promise you.' Clive pursed his lips, unwilling to confide in his granddaughter. If his gamble paid off, there'd be plenty of money to pay for the party. And if it didn't, well, he wouldn't be around to worry about it, and the party would have to be cancelled.

Seven days later, Clive was a bag of nerves. All week he'd been frightened to do anything. If he went out, he might trip off the kerb and fall under a bus. If he stayed in, his boiler might explode and finish him off. Or maybe he'd just have a straight-forward heart attack. Oh, when you stopped to think about it, there were altogether too many ways to die. Willis's didn't need to send thugs to do the job!

At last the great day had arrived, and with it, the most mail Clive had ever received. He sorted through the cards and letters eagerly, looking for that most special envelope of all, the one with Her Majesty's coat of arms on. He wasn't disappointed.

As soon as he'd opened the post, he got ready to go out. The party wasn't until the afternoon – Mia was coming to collect him at two. Plenty of time to get his finances in order first.

Clive put on his coat, and retrieved the folder of documents he'd sorted out months ago, in preparation for today. There'd been many times when he'd thought he wouldn't make it, but here he was.

It was a short walk to Willis's. Even at Clive's pace, with his Zimmer frame, it only took ten minutes.

At the bookmakers, Clive handed over his slip, along with his birth certificate and his passport.

'I've come to collect my winnings,' he announced proudly to the cashier. 'I'm one hundred today. One hundred pounds, at two hundred and fifty to one. I'll take a cheque, please.'

He enjoyed the look of astonishment on the cashier's face, as she examined his documents. Then she smiled broadly at him, and began to clap. Soon everyone in the branch of Willis's were applauding, staff and punters alike, and Clive grinned with pleasure. He couldn't wait to tell Mia and the rest of his family about the bet. It was going to be his best birthday ever.

The End

The Bet – Discussion

A gentle little story, category 2 or 3. Inspired by a true story in which a man placed a bet that he'd reach his 100th birthday when he was 80. I read the article about him in *The Weekly News*, wrote the story and sold it back to them. Now that's what I call recycling!

Reading this one back, I've just noticed I used the name Clive again for an old man. Clive turned up in *The Missing Piece*, and again here. I quite often do this. In my head there's a stock of characters of different types, and I pull them out and use them. The two Clives might not be quite the same person but as soon as I add a Clive to a story I have a good picture of him. I've also got Claire and Kirsty who we met in *High Fliers* and who tend to crop up over and over again in my stories. It's a kind of short cut. If you have some ready-developed characters you'll be able to get going with a new story idea more quickly.

And the more you write, the better at writing you'll become. The more you submit, the better your chances of publication. Only one thing is certain in the womag story writing world: you've got to sub it to pub it.

Rejection

An ugly word, but one we'd better have a quick chat about. If you submit stories to magazines, some of them will be rejected. That's a given, I'm afraid. There are no womag writers who sell everything they write. Even the top writers, whose names you'll see every week in the magazines, get their share of rejections. In fact, as they tend to write and submit more than anyone else, they probably get more rejections in terms of actual numbers, than anyone else.

One top writer I know once phoned an editor to discuss a serial she was writing for them, and while on the phone casually asked for news of her short stories currently under consideration. *Twelve* verbal rejections later, she wished she hadn't. Ouch.

Similarly, if you've been submitting to UK magazines for a while you'll have experienced the horror of *Take A Break*'s regular clear-out days. The staff at *Take A Break* seem to have a habit of sending large numbers of rejections out at the same time. All writers can do is console each other on those days, and remember that soon after the clear-out days come the acceptance days, so if they've still got one of your stories, you can live on in hope…

But don't worry about rejection. A rejection means you got that far. You wrote a story, edited it, researched a market, submitted it. It was considered, but was not chosen. Maybe the editor had just bought a story with a similar theme. Maybe they had enough stories of that particular length. Maybe the story isn't quite good enough, in which case rewrite it before sending it out again. As it says on a tea-towel I recently bought from author Nicola Morgan's online shop (www.nicolamorgan.com/shop), Don't be bitter, be better.

A rejection is not the end of the road. In fact, let's not call them rejections. Let's call them, in womag-writer Rosie Edser's words, 're-marketing opportunities'. There, that's put a more positive spin on things, hasn't it?

If a rejection gets you down, I prescribe wine, chocolate or your comforter of choice, take a day off and then begin work on a new story. As author Joe Konrath said, There's a word for a writer who never gives up: Published.

On that note, let's have another story. One which was never rejected. I'm fond of this story – it won a writing class competition and then was published by *Take A Break*. It's one I felt quietly proud of from the moment I finished it. That doesn't often happen.

Finding Mum

I make a place my own by painting it. I always have, since I was a small girl. When I swapped to a bigger bedroom, I drew detailed pictures of it and pinned them to the walls. When I changed schools, I sketched the classroom. When I left home and bought my own flat, I painted pictures of every room from every angle.

I'm painting a picture of the kitchen today. I'm hoping it'll help me turn it into *my* kitchen. It's not a particularly attractive room so I've put a basket of vegetables on the table to add colour and give a better focus. Otherwise the picture will show nothing but ugly brown Seventies units. They were here when I last drew this room, thirty years ago. I'd have used crayons then, rather than oils; I was only five.

It's not been easy, painting the house this time around. Too many memories. I struggled with the living room and hallway, then decided to tackle the kitchen. Mum's domain.

Now, I sketch in the table, and begin to add detail to the basket of vegetables. Carrots, onions, leafy celery. A nice bit of still life. Mum always liked celery leaves, I remember suddenly. Most people would cut them off and throw them away, but Mum would add them to the salads, or finely chop them and sprinkle them on new potatoes.

'Best bit of the plant, that,' she'd say. 'And no sense throwing it away if you can eat it.'

She'd grown up in the war years. Waste not, want not, make do and mend. I'd hated that attitude when I was in my teens. Couldn't wait to move out, get my own place, become part of the Eighties throwaway society. I bought ready-washed celery in Marks and Spencer. It didn't come with leaves on.

I start on the units behind the table in the picture. There was once a fireplace there, but the chimney was blocked off and the space used to house a boiler before I was born. I squeeze some white paint onto the palette to add the boiler, and then stop. It'd look a lot better if I paint the fireplace as it would have been, before the ugly boiler was installed. There was once a range cooker here, its flue making use of the chimney. Mum used to talk about it – endlessly during those long days while I sat at her side and listened to her talk in such detail, with such animation, about the past. Then she'd turn to me and say, 'And who are you, dear?'

I decide to paint an old-fashioned range. Blackened cast iron. I add some shiny saucepans and a kettle on the hob. The brown seventies units I started on look all wrong, so I paint them out.

When Mum was a girl, the kitchen walls were part tiled, part whitewash over lime plaster. She used to help with the food preparation.

'I should have been a professional cook, you know,' she would say when I visited her in the home. 'Like that Fanny Cradock. She was on the television last night. Did you see her?'

Last century, more like, I thought. But I told her what she wanted to hear.

'Yes, Mum. I saw her. Your cooking is far better than hers, though.'

Wrong thing to say. She closed up.

'How would you know what my cooking's like? And why do you call me mum? I don't know you.'

And I don't know you either, any more, I thought sadly.

There's a gap in my painting. The vegetables aren't working as the main point of interest. There's too much wall space. Before I quite know what I'm doing I start to outline a figure – a woman, dressed in a 1940s plain dress and pinafore. She's cooking, her hands are deep in a bowl, mixing dough. It's as though I can see her, standing there in front of me, yet sixty years in the past. I stop thinking about what I'm doing and let the brush move over the canvas, her form taking shape under my fingers.

It was a relief of a kind, when Mum died. There was nothing of *her* left any more. Just a weakening shell, and snippets of ancient memories which would bubble to the surface now and then; less and less often as the days went on. It had been painful to visit her for some time, and yet I had to go – every two days – and sit with her for an hour. She was still my mum.

I'm working on the face now. Her hair is brown, short and bobbed, parted at the side and held with a Kirby grip. Her face is gentle and serene. She's absorbed in what she's doing, hardly aware of the artist sitting across the table from her. She seems so real to me now. I half expect her to look up and smile.

If she did, I'd see her eyes. That startling piercing blue. She never lost that colour – her eyes kept their intensity until the day she died. Her gaze could be quite unnerving. She seemed able to look right into your soul, even when she could no longer recognise her own daughter.

She was in the nursing home for seven years, but always refused to sell the house. Even in the final stages, it was the one thing she was always clear about. She was born here, in the front bedroom. So was I.

'I lived all my life in that house, you know,' she'd say. 'It's where my kitchen is, where I belong.' She would look past me then, at people and places only she could see. And I knew I would have to keep the old house.

It took me two months to come back. And another month before I brought my easel and began the paintings. I thought it would take several more weeks before I'd feel able to move in, before I could impose my things, my style and my clutter in my mother's house.

Now I put the final touches to my picture. There's a tiny smile playing around the corners of her mouth. She seems happy, and so am I, now that I've found her, living on in the memories of this house. I decide to move in tomorrow.

The End

Finding Mum – Discussion

I rate this as a category 5 story – an emotional one. It is of course a 'coming to terms' story. My unnamed main character likes to paint pictures of rooms she lives in, and by painting the kitchen of her mother's old house as it would have been when her mother was young, she is able to come to terms with her mother's decline and passing. The inspiration for this story was a painting – you can probably imagine what the painting was of: a woman in a 1940s pinafore, hands deep in a mixing bowl, standing at a table laden with fresh vegetables. (The picture was the prompt for a writing class competition. If you're stuck for ideas, flick through a weekend colour supplement, choose a photo and try writing the story behind it.)

When I began writing this one I had in mind it would be a ghost story – the ghost of Mum would guide the painter's hand. At that time I was writing a lot of ghost stories, but as I wrote it, I realised it didn't need a supernatural element. Although Mum seems to materialise in the painting, she's not a ghost, she's a memory, and by painting her, her daughter is allowing her memory to live on in the house.

Sometimes this happens – a good idea for a story becomes a better idea as you write it. In this case I needed to hold back and keep the story understated. Other times, you might have ideas of elements to add to the story while you write it. Go with this – trust your instinct. Don't hold too tightly to your first idea as it might not be the best one. Or if you're not sure whether the new idea is better or worse, consider writing two versions, then see which works best. This is a particularly good tip for beginner writers. As you become more experienced, you'll learn to spot which are the best ideas as they occur.

Sometimes, you only have half an idea, and you just can't work out what the end of the story should be. Too often those half-written stories end up abandoned in a dusty corner of your hard-drive. But if the initial idea is good, don't give up on it. This next story was one where I wrote half, liked what I'd written but was completely stuck for an ending. Read it, then I'll tell you how I managed to finish it. Originally published in *My Weekly*.

Did I Hit An Angel?

'What do you mean, you think you hit an angel?' Gary frowned at Nina. She waved her hands vaguely.

'I don't know, it came from nowhere, and bounced off my windscreen.' Nina plucked a tissue from a box and blew her nose. She knew there was little hope of Gary believing her. She barely believed it herself.

'An angel? Like, with wings and a halo?' said Gary.

'It was small, white and fluttery. I didn't see a halo.'

'Then it was probably a plastic bag, blowing around in the wind.'

'There are white feathers caught under the windscreen wipers.'

'A bird, then?'

Nina looked away. 'I saw its face as it bounced off the car. *Her* face, that is.'

Gary laughed, shook his head and turned on the TV. 'Um, Nina, sorry.' He gestured towards the TV with the remote. 'Football's started. Tell me about it later, OK?'

Nina began to shred her tissue, letting the little white pieces flutter down onto the floor. It *was* an angel she'd hit, she was sure of it. It had been a horrible drive home; lashing rain and high winds, and the lanes around the village were dark and high-hedged. As she'd rounded a bend, the angel had suddenly appeared, fluttering around head height in the middle of the lane. There'd been no chance of swerving to avoid it. A soft bump, a glimpse of a tiny, terrified face, and then it was gone.

Now she didn't understand why she hadn't stopped to look for it. The poor thing was probably lying injured, maybe even dying, by the roadside. Was it even possible to kill an angel, Nina wondered? At the time she'd been so shocked it had taken all her efforts to keep the car on the road and not in a hedge. Once she was back in control, the rational part of her brain kept telling her it must have been a bird, or a piece of litter, just as Gary had suggested. But the more she thought about it now, the more sure she was that she'd hit an angel.

'They're very small, you know. Smaller than most people imagine,' she said.

'What are?' Gary asked. His eyes stayed focussed on the football.

'Angels,' Nina replied.

'Oh for goodness sake,' Gary said, turning the TV sound up.

Nina took that as a cue for her to leave the room. She didn't blame Gary for not believing her, but she did wish he'd listen to her. After all, she'd had a shock, and almost crashed the car. A little sympathy wouldn't have gone amiss.

She went upstairs and decided to get ready for bed. Her soft satin nightie slid smoothly down over her body and clung to her legs. Its floaty white fabric made her think again of the angel – picturing its terrified face and hearing the soft thump of impact. Perhaps it was someone's guardian angel. If she'd really hurt it, what would that mean for the person it watched over? Were their lives connected? Could the human go on living without the angel?

Realising she would never get to sleep without

knowing for certain, Nina went back downstairs and slipped her cream jacket over her nightie. Gary was still watching TV. There was no point telling him where she was going – he would think she was mad. She took her car keys and went out to look for the angel.

As she approached the bend where she'd hit it, Nina slowed the car to a crawl. It was still raining heavily, and she could see nothing in the car headlights.

'Oh this is stupid,' she muttered, peering through the rain. 'There's nothing here. I should go home.' But as she pulled the car into a field gateway to turn around she saw something move under the hedge.

'A rabbit, I guess. Suppose I should check it out, now I've come this far.' She climbed out of the car, wincing as the cold rain instantly soaked through her flimsy nightdress.

'Hello?' she called. 'Is someone there?'

'Help me, please, help me! I think I've broken my leg, and my shoulder's killing me!'

It was not the voice of a dainty angel. Nina bent down to look the ditch, and saw a young cyclist, his legs tangled awkwardly in his bent bicycle, his clothes soaked through, his face pale.

'Oh goodness, what happened?' she cried, kneeling beside him in the mud.

'I don't know, I must have hit a pothole or something, one minute I had my head down, cycling against the wind, next minute I was in the ditch. Ow, my leg! Can you call an ambulance?'

Nina patted her jacket pockets, but they were empty. Idiot! Never leave the house without your phone, Gary was always telling her.

'Um, I don't have a phone. I think there's a farmhouse somewhere near…'

'Please don't leave me!' The young man grabbed Nina's hand and held tight.

'OK, I won't leave you. What's your name?'

'Ben, I'm Ben. I was on my way home. Been playing soccer…'

Rain trickled down the back of Nina's neck. She shivered. Ben must be freezing, as well as being in huge pain. 'I've got a rug in the car – let me get it for you,' she said, gently extricating her hand.

Nina ran over to her car to get the rug. Ben needed to get to hospital quickly. Perhaps she could help him to her car, drive him there herself. Back at his side, she wrapped the blanket around his upper body, hoping it would keep the worst of the rain off him. Then she began trying to lift the bicycle off his legs, but one leg was bent at an odd angle around the crossbar, and she didn't dare move it too much.

'Ben, I can't move you, but you need to go to hospital. I'll have to drive to a phone. I'll be as quick as I can, I promise.'

'No, no, don't go.' His voice was barely more than a whisper now. 'Angel, my angel.'

Nina frowned. What was he saying about angels? She couldn't leave him in this state, and she knew she mustn't let him lose consciousness. She held his hand and began to chat to him, asking him questions about his soccer team, his home, his family. Maybe they'd be lucky, and some late-night driver would come past…

A flash of headlights and the throb of a car's engine were the sweetest things Nina had ever seen or heard. She leapt up, shouting and waving. 'Help, help! Please stop! Here!' The car stopped in the middle of the lane, its driver jumped out of the car and ran to her, leaving the door open.

'Nina, thank goodness, you're ok! You're drenched.

What's happened?' It was Gary. Nina sobbed with relief and pointed over to where Ben lay.

'I found him, in the ditch. He's injured. Call an ambulance, oh Gary, you do have your phone with you, don't you?'

'Of course, but who's injured? Not your angel?' Gary peered into the dark hedgerow and gasped when he saw Ben. He called an ambulance while Nina went back to the cyclist's side.

'Ben, hold on.' She held his hand tightly. 'An ambulance is on its way. It'll be ok now. Just hang on in there, Ben.'

Later, home again, and wrapped in warm blankets, Nina sipped a mug of hot chocolate and looked at Gary.

'So what I don't understand is, when you realised I'd gone out, what made you drive down that lane to look for me?'

'Well,' Gary smiled, 'you won't believe this but it was the angel.'

'What? You've seen her too?'

'Course not! I saw the little pile of shredded tissue you left on the sofa, and remembered what you'd said about hitting an angel on the lane. So I guessed you'd gone looking for it, my crazy, wonderful woman. And there you were.'

'Ben, the cyclist, was muttering something about angels too. I think maybe he saw the same one I saw. Perhaps that's why he crashed.'

'No, love. He crashed because he hit a massive pothole. I saw it, right on the bend. And the only angel he saw was you – ministering to him in your white nightie, like you were his guardian angel. You've probably saved his life, Nina. I'm proud of you. And I promise I won't laugh at you next time you come home with some mad story.'

Nina smiled and snuggled up against her husband on the sofa. Ben may well have hit a pothole, but his guardian angel had brought him help when he needed it, she was certain of that.

The End

Did I Hit An Angel – Discussion

I'm glad I could include a supernatural story in this book. If you've read my ghost stories book you'll know how much I enjoy a little bit of unexplained magic. I'd have included this story in the other book, but angels aren't ghosts so it didn't quite fit. We'll talk more about supernatural stories in a minute but first I promised to tell you how I found an ending for this one.

My first draft had got to the point where Nina is upstairs getting ready for bed, fretting about the poor injured angel, wondering if she should go back out and look for it. And then I was stuck. I really did not know where to go next. So I took it along to my writing class and read it out. Everyone loved the beginning, and we quickly got into a brainstorming session about what could happen next. Then someone said, what if she does go back out and finds a cyclist in the ditch? I knew instantly that was the right thing to do, the perfect way to progress the story. Sometimes you can't work all alone – you need input from other writers. If you can, join a writing class or group, or a good online group. It'll give you no end of help, encouragement and inspiration.

My writing tutor, Della Galton, had more advice. She liked the details of Nina's shredded tissue and slinky white nightie, but said I should only keep those details in if they were important to the story. There had to be a point to them – they couldn't be there just as fancy prose, there's no space in a short story for that. So I made the shredded tissue act as the clue for Gary to guess where Nina had gone, and the nightie allowed Ben to think Nina was an angel. When I'd finished writing, I knew I had a satisfying story where every detail did its job. I've sold this one twice – after *My Weekly* it was republished in the Australian magazine *That's Life: Fast Fiction*.

Make good use of description

I've never forgotten that advice about making use of detail. It's lovely to include little pieces of description, but don't just put them there for the sake of it. Make them do two jobs – describe the setting or the action and *also* hint at mood, or add to the plot as I did in this story. For instance, if your character is walking along a woodland path, and you want to include some description, then do. But make sure your description adds to the story. If your character is sad and depressed, she'll be looking down at her feet. Describe the muddy path, the dead, fallen leaves, cold rain dripping down the back of her neck. If she's happy and cheerful and having a good day, describe the dappled sunshine, the trees breaking into bud, riotous birdsong. Don't *tell* us her mood, but use your description of what she observes to *show* us it.

Supernatural stories

When writing a story with a supernatural element, give yourself the best chance of success by trying to ensure the story has an alternative rational explanation. Although some magazines will publish stories which are in-your-face ghost stories with no other way to explain the action, others prefer stories which can be enjoyed by sceptics. In *Did I Hit An Angel?* I had Nina believe in angels and Gary as the voice of reason, telling her it was a plastic bag she hit, and that Ben's mutterings about angels was just because Nina was standing over him in her white nightie. Readers can choose which explanation they prefer. By using your characters to discuss what happened you can easily put forward the two opposing explanations.

It's not always possible to come up with an alternative rational explanation but if you can, you'll probably end up with a story that appeals to a wider market. If you want to write a proper ghost story, make sure you:

- Know and explain why the ghost is active now, haunting your characters in this location at this time.

- Give the ghost a problem which needs to be resolved before it can rest in peace, and resolve the ghost's problem along with the main character's problem. Actually the MC's problem is probably that he or she is being haunted by a ghost…

- Decide on your rules for ghosts – can they walk through walls? Can they be seen or only heard? – and stick to them consistently throughout the story.

If you like the idea of writing ghost stories, please do consider reading my book, *Ghost Stories and How to Write Them,* which gives plenty of examples and discusses what makes a good womag ghost story in a lot of depth.

Other Writers

I couldn't have completed *Did I Hit An Angel?* without some input from my fellow writers. Gone are the days when writers closeted themselves in garrets and wrote alone. These days with writing classes and circles in most towns, online forums and Facebook groups there's no need to think of writing as a lonely occupation. Sure, while you're deep into first draft or editing only you can do it, but in between, find other writers to socialise with either in the flesh or online. It makes it a much more rewarding occupation. Other writers can help you get out of plot holes, or get over writer's block, or give you feedback on whether a story's working or not. I go to a weekly writing class which never ceases to be inspirational, and I'm a member of some online and Facebook writers' groups. If I'd never met any other writers, I'm sure I'd have given up long ago.

Some of my writer friends, whom I originally met via the internet, are now my best friends. No one understands it all better than they do!

And no one offers a better shoulder to cry on when my story fails to sell.

The Ones Which Didn't Sell

I'm being very brave here. I'm going to bare my soul and include a couple of stories which I never managed to sell. They're not *bad* stories – I wouldn't dare inflict my really rubbish ones on you, dear reader! They're stories I felt were good enough to submit, but which were declined by the magazine editors. With the benefit of a few more years experience I think I know why, and I've included my thoughts after each story.

But what do *you* think? Would you have bought them? Let's play at being magazine editors. Put your critical head on and decide why these stories weren't good enough to publish in the womags.

Acceptance

We had forty minutes to get dressed. I couldn't believe we'd left it that late, but we'd been rushing about all morning making sure the preparations were in hand. Eventually Gordon had grabbed me by the hand and pulled me upstairs.

'They can take care of everything else by themselves, Ali,' he'd said. 'Come on, we need some time to get ourselves sorted out.'

He'd already nabbed the shower, so I busied myself laying out my dress, shoes and hat – got to wear a hat! – so that it was all ready for me to put on. He was right, too. We needed time, not just to get washed and dressed, but to think this whole thing through. It's not that we were uncertain about it any more. But we needed to talk it over, one last time, and draw a line under our misgivings.

'Come on, Gordon!' I banged on the door to the en-suite. 'Must be my turn now.' He appeared, wrapped in a towel.

'Sorry. All yours,' he said, running his fingers through his damp hair. 'So, are you looking forward to being a dreaded mother-in-law? Awful creatures, they are.'

I thumped him as I passed. 'I'll be a fab mother-in-law. I'll break the stereotype, and you know it!'

The shower was warm and comforting. I told myself it

was washing away the old Ali – the one who worried her son was making the wrong choices and taking the hard road through life.

It only seemed like yesterday that Ned was a baby, taking his first steps, speaking his first words. 'Clock!' he'd said, pointing to one on my mother's wall. Gordon and I looked at each other and laughed. We'd placed bets on whether 'Mama' or 'Dada' would be his first word, but he'd chosen his own word and surprised us. A taste of what was to come.

I shampooed my hair, reduced the temperature a little and turned my face upwards into the refreshing monsoon. I remembered Ned standing under a waterfall once, arms outstretched, face tilted up. I thought then that he was the most beautiful child who ever lived.

He was an easy, if independent-spirited, boy to bring up. Into sport – mostly swimming and athletics, a big reader, an average academic. There was a phase in his teens I preferred not to think about too deeply. Black spiked hair, torn black clothes, and – briefly – a nose-piercing. Gordon wanted to insist he took the stud out, but I persuaded him to let things be, wait for Ned to decide to remove it himself.

It didn't last too long. By the time Ned left home he was the nicest, smartest, most polite young man you could ever hope to meet.

I wrapped myself in a soft white towel, and wiped the steamed-up mirror. I looked clean, but old. Still, there was half an hour to transform myself. As mother of the groom, I had to look my best. I wondered what Casey's mum would wear. She'd seemed more glamorous than me, on the one occasion Ned and Casey took us to meet her.

Back in the bedroom, Gordon was buttoning his shirt. I combed my hair through, and gave it a quick blast with the hairdryer.

'Do you remember,' said Gordon, as he pulled on a pair of socks, 'that first girlfriend Ned brought home?'

'Caroline. Or Carol? Something like that.' I realised I could hardly remember a thing about her.

'That's the one. You could tell, couldn't you – she was so wrong for him.'

That was the only thing I did remember about her. That she and Ned seemed not to fit, in any way. I'd been glad when they split up. It hadn't lasted long.

'Then there was Michelle,' I said.

'I didn't meet her,' Gordon said. 'You didn't like her, did you?'

'Not much.' Not at all, as I remembered. There'd been a long gap after that, when Ned lived alone, brought no one to meet us, and didn't mention anyone special. Until Casey came along.

'Tell me again,' said Gordon. 'What did you think when Ned brought Casey to meet us that first time.'

I laughed. We'd talked about this so many times over the last five years. We'd dissected every minute of that meeting, pored over in miniscule detail what we'd said and how we'd felt. It had been a balmy summer evening. Gordon and I had been sitting in the garden when Ned and Casey arrived.

I turned the hairdryer off for a moment. 'First I thought there was some mistake,' I said. 'This couldn't possibly be the person Ned was always talking about.'

'Your mouth dropped open when he introduced you,' said Gordon, smiling.

'So did yours! But I recovered pretty quickly, I thought.'

'Not bad, not bad,' agreed Gordon. He'd done a reasonable job himself, as I recalled. He'd shaken Casey's hand, offered a drink, then disappeared inside to fetch a bottle of wine. I think it was only me who'd noticed the slight stumble as he stepped through the patio door, and the tiny disbelieving shake of his head.

That night, after they'd left, we talked for hours. Gordon shouted. I cried. We drank a lot. We'd both seen that this relationship was something special, but neither of us mentioned that, at the time.

It was hard, remembering how I'd felt that night.

My hair was done. Time for some make-up. Gordon had put his suit on, and was peering over my shoulder into the mirror as he knotted his tie. 'I liked Casey, from the start,' he said.

I smiled and kept quiet. You wouldn't have guessed it, from what he'd said that night after the first meeting.

Ned had phoned us the next day. 'Thanks Mum. You were great, both of you. I didn't know how you'd react, Casey being – well, I guess not what you were expecting.'

'Casey's lovely,' I'd said, and was surprised to find I meant it.

'Thing is, Mum,' he'd said, stammering. 'I-I'm in love.' But I already knew that, in my heart.

I pushed Gordon out of the way so I could have a better view as I applied my lipstick. A gorgeous deep plum, to match my dress.

'The thing that upset me,' Gordon said, 'is that however nice a person Casey is, this isn't what I'd dreamt of for our son. Do you know what I mean?'

I did know. You have these pictures in your head, don't you, of how your kids' lives will pan out. You imagine your son with a pretty young girl, marrying when he's about 30, after he's seen a bit of the world. Grandkids coming along within a few years – three of them, all blonde and bouncy. A succession of houses, each one a little bigger and better than the last, until they settle down not too far from you, and you can babysit for them when needed.

I caught hold of Gordon's hand, and brushed away a single tear. Our eyes met in the mirror. He was worried I'd cry. But I'd done my grieving - for the life Ned wouldn't now lead, the grandchildren who wouldn't be born.

This wasn't a day for tears. It was a day for pride. Pride for the way our son had known who he was and what he wanted, and had found his own way. And pride in ourselves. Because Ned had known he could bring Casey to our house and knew we'd be welcoming.

'We did well, didn't we, bringing Ned up?' I said, to Gordon's reflection.

'We did, indeed. He's a fine young man,' he said, bending to kiss my cheek. 'Come on now. Ten minutes to go, and you're not in your frock yet!'

My outfit was a soft plum silk dress with matching jacket. It'd cost a bomb, but as Gordon said when I'd brought it home, we'd only the one son.

And there would only be the one wedding. He'd found his partner for life – of that I was now sure.

It wasn't a traditional church do. Just the local registry office, and then dinner at the best hotel in town. They'd hired a band, and there was to be a party afterwards with all their friends.

I slipped my shoes onto my feet and my hat on my head, and stood in front of the mirror.

'Not bad,' said Gordon. 'In fact, I'd go so far as to say you look fantastic!' I smiled, the proud smile of a loving mother, on her son's big day.

I wondered again about Casey's mother. I hoped she felt as proud as I did, on *her* son's big day. Soon we'd see the two of them, shoulder to shoulder in front of the registrar, promising themselves to each other for all time. Two men, perfectly matched.

'They're soul mates, you know,' said Gordon, quietly.

'I know,' I replied.

It was time to go downstairs now, and make sure everyone else was ready. I took a deep breath and Gordon's arm, and off we went.

The End

Acceptance – Discussion

Unfortunately the title wasn't prophetic, and this story never got an acceptance despite several outings. On the surface, there's nothing really wrong with it. It has lots of emotion, an uplifting ending with a twist, a nice structure, sympathetic characters, and though I say it myself, it's pretty well-written. And yet it was rejected by several magazines. Why do you think that is?

I'm certain now, that I know the reason.

While it is acceptable to have homosexual characters in your stories, there does seem to be a golden rule for womag stories – *don't make their sexuality the point or the twist of the story.* By all means write a story in which the main characters *happen* to be gay, but ensure the story works even if you'd made them straight. Don't write a story which points its finger at your characters' sexual preferences. Which of course this one does, by using that fact as the twist. Note that if I removed the twist, we'd end up with a 'so what' story. The end would leave the reader wondering what the point of the story was. Stories need to stand up in their own right even without their twist endings. This one doesn't.

I also fell into the gender-twist trap of needing to

come up with an ambiguous name for one of my characters. I remember trying several (Alex, Bobbi, Georgie) before deciding on Casey. These days I think you'd initially consider Casey to be a girl's name, which is what I needed you to think, but of course there was the legendary American railroad man, Casey Jones.

When writing it I was trying to make the reader think of other reasons why Ben's choice of partner might not be all his parents had hoped for him – perhaps she was older, or from a different culture, or disabled in some way. Actually I think if I had gone for any of those reasons as the twist, the story still wouldn't have sold. Because there's a risk of giving offence – the story as it stands could offend gay people (and I do apologise if any readers of this book found it offensive in any way, but I've included it to make a point). If my 'twist' had been that Casey was wheelchair-bound and unable to bear children, the story could have upset disabled people or their carers. If she'd been black and Ben's parents were white – well, let's not even go there.

Including an identity twist can add a lot to a story as discussed earlier, but you do have to be super-careful how you handle it. I got it wrong in this story, which I wrote several years ago. I know better now.

Let's move on. This next story was rejected a couple of times, but I rather like it anyway.

Aunt Martha's Secrets

The box of Aunt Martha's possessions, forwarded by the care home after her death, was paltry. Sarah couldn't believe how little there was. She'd told the home to get rid of her aunt's clothes, but to send everything else on to her. She'd been expecting a small van load, but there was only a single cardboard box.

In it were a handful of books, a small jewellery box containing plastic beads, a padlock key on a key ring shaped like the letter J, and a tarnished silver crucifix. There was also a battered leather handbag and purse containing £5.47, and some clay sculptures.

'Is that it, Aunt Martha?' Sarah said. 'Is that all you've left, after a lifetime of 80 years?'

She picked up the crucifix and peered at it. 'I still don't know you, yet I'm all you had – your only living relative and sole beneficiary, for what it's worth. For goodness sake, I only met you once, and that must be thirty years ago!'

She'd been sixteen, in the throes of 'O' level revision, the only time she'd met Aunt Martha. Sarah had felt weighed down with worry over the impending exams, and had felt the need to get away. She told her parents she was going to stay with a school friend.

Looking back, she realised it was a typical teenage

rebellion – running away to the aunt she'd always known she had, but whom she'd never met. Her father would say nothing about his sister, except that she was a talented artist. And her mother would just purse her mouth and say, 'she's not a good woman, that Martha. Not someone you'd want to know.'

Sarah had found Martha's phone number in her father's address book, and promised herself that some day she'd use the number and track down her aunt, visiting her in the sunny seaside town where she'd made her home. She'd imagined the reunion countless times – sometimes joyful, sometimes tearful, but always a meeting of similar souls.

'You're the only one who understands me,' she pictured herself saying over mugs of hot chocolate and slices of fudge cake. Aunt Martha would sigh and take her hand. 'And you, me.'

But that's not how it went, Sarah remembered, as she twirled the chain of the crucifix around her fingers. They'd met in the station coffee shop as arranged. Sarah had imagined a tall, glamorous, artistically-dressed woman. But Martha turned out to be small and mousy, with a worn expression and suspicious eyes.

She looked at Sarah appraisingly. 'Well, my girl. So you've run away to your long lost aunt, have you? There's a train back at 4pm, you'll be on that. Meanwhile, we've three hours to get to know each other.'

It was a strange day. Martha bought her lunch, then took her to the beach where they strolled along the promenade eating ice-creams. But throughout, Aunt Martha treated Sarah coolly, keeping her at arm's length. More like a policewoman accompanying an errant teenager home, than an aunt meeting her only niece for the first time, Sarah thought.

'Why don't you ever come to visit us?' she asked.

'Hmm, that's a question I think your father could answer far better than me.' Sarah detected a sneer in her aunt's voice.

She clammed up then, and set her face hard. Sarah licked her ice-cream and walked in silence beside her aunt. Almost at the end of the prom, Martha stopped, turned her back on the sea and stared at a beach hut.

'I should get it painted,' she murmured.

'Is it yours?' Sarah asked, running over and tugging at the door.

'Don't open that door!' Martha hissed, pulling Sarah away. 'Whatever you do, keep away from that hut!'

'Why? If it's yours, why can't we go in?'

'Because we can't. It's mine. My private place to be with Jack.'

'Who's Jack?'

Martha clammed up again. 'Come on, my girl. We need to get going or you'll miss your train.'

Sarah had been glad to get back home that day. She'd found her parents in the kitchen, beginning to worry where she was, after her cover-story friend had phoned looking for her.

'Where've you *been*?' said her mother, screwing up a wet tissue.

'I went to visit Aunt Martha,' she said.

'Martha! But why?' asked her father.

'Because she's my aunt,' Sarah said stubbornly. 'And I've a right to know her.'

'And now that you've met her?'

'She's, well, she's a bit odd,' said Sarah. 'Who's Jack?'

Her parents both paled. Her mother began tearing her tissue into shreds, and looked at Sarah's father to answer.

'Jack is, well, Jack *was*, Martha's husband,' he explained. 'He'd become my best friend, too.'

'What happened to him?'

'We don't know.'

Her mother snorted. 'But we *suspect*.'

'Suspect what?'

Her father sighed. 'They went on holiday, Jack and Martha. They'd been married just one year, and it wasn't working out – so it seemed to us. They were always having rows.'

'Jack never came back from that holiday,' said Sarah's mother.

'He swam out to sea, got caught in a rip tide. But there was only Martha's word for what happened. No one else saw. They never found the body.'

Sarah's mother sighed. 'Poor Jack. He was such a lovely man. But Martha - she was so inconsistent. Every time she told the story it was different. And you know what *I* think happened on that holiday.'

Her father had frowned at Sarah's mother. 'That's enough. You're scaring the girl.'

Jack. Of course, that was what the J on the key ring stood for. Jack, who her parents had liked so much, that when he disappeared they would no longer have anything to do with Martha. Sarah picked up the key, and turned it over in her hands. But what did it open?

Suddenly she noticed something scratched onto the body of the key. A number, 359. *My private place to be with Jack.* Her aunt's words returned clearly to her. Perhaps this was the key to the beach hut?

There was only one way to find out.

The following weekend, Sarah took a train to the seaside town. It was a grey, cold day – the holiday season was long over. She zipped up her fleece jacket, thrust her hands into her pockets and walked down the hill to the beach. A row of brightly coloured beach huts stretched along the promenade in both directions. She set off to the far end, hunching her shoulders against the wind.

When she found the hut, it was in a bad state of repair - the paint was peeling and the wood rotting. It was one of a line of six, all in poor condition. A notice attached to a nearby lamppost announced that the council intended to replace these huts with new ones. Leaseholders were advised to have their huts cleared of personal possessions by the end of the month.

Sarah took the key out of her pocket and approached the hut. The lock was rusty, and she needed to jiggle the key around to get it in, but it fitted. She heard her aunt's voice in her head again: *Don't open that door!*

Her parents whispered suspicions came back to her. *They never found the body. You know what I think.*

What did they think, exactly? That Martha had done away with her husband and hidden his body? Where? Buried him in the garden or…

Suddenly the rust gave way and the padlock snapped open.

Whatever you do, keep away from that hut.

Sarah shivered, and not from the cold wind, as she pulled the door.

As it creaked open, the smell of something rotten assaulted her senses. Oh God, what if her parents were right, and Martha had hidden Jack's body here? She retched, shaking uncontrollably, but forced herself to step inside, peering around until her eyes adjusted to the gloomy interior.

There was a scrap of threadbare carpet on the floor, a shelf holding some mildewed books, and a frayed armchair, placed facing inwards. A curtain separated the hut into two sections. Taking a deep breath, Sarah pulled it aside to reveal the far end.

She gasped.

A large old-fashioned sideboard stood across the back wall. Arranged on it were framed photographs of a young man and a woman Sarah recognised as Aunt Martha. In the middle, in pride of place, was a head.

It was so life-like, and such a good likeness of the man in the photos, that for a fraction of a second Sarah thought it was real. Sighing with relief she carefully picked up the sculpture.

It was beautifully made and intricately detailed. She turned it around, admiring the work that had gone into shaping the lobes of the ears, the flare of the nostrils, the faint laughter lines around the eyes. This was a work of true and enduring love, not the work of a murderer, surely?

Placing it back amongst the photos, she sat down in the armchair for a moment and gazed at the photos.

That sideboard they were on. It was an odd piece of furniture for a beach hut. Six feet long, and two feet wide. Big enough to hold a… Sarah jumped up, her hand flew to her mouth. No, surely her aunt wouldn't have, couldn't have…

She took several deep breaths. Her instinct was to leave the beach hut, throw the key into the waves and run away, far from here. Let the council demolish the hut and Aunt Martha's secrets with it. Sarah would rather not know.

And end up like Mum and Dad? A voice niggled at the back of her head. Her parents had made up their minds on no evidence that Martha had murdered Jack. Now, although they were long gone Sarah had a chance to prove them right, or wrong.

She only had to open the sideboard doors.

She crouched down and steeled herself. 'OK, Sarah, you can do this.' Taking hold of the cupboard door handles she pulled them open quickly.

Inside was a pile of men's clothes and a box of papers. No body. Sarah sighed with relief, although it still didn't prove her parents were wrong about Martha.

She picked up the box of papers and leafed through them. They seemed to be letters, to Martha and signed, simply, 'J'. Sarah scanned through them quickly, her mouth falling open with astonishment as her aunt's secrets revealed themselves bit by bit with every letter.

The letters were from Jack. Martha's husband, and her father's best friend, had apparently been a wanted criminal. He'd embezzled a large amount of money from the bank he worked for, over several years.

'That's what their rows must have been about,' Sarah whispered. 'She must have hated knowing she was living on stolen money.'

She looked at the dates on the letters. They spanned two decades, from the fifties to the seventies. She read some more. When it looked as though he was going to be found out, he and Martha had come up with the plan to fake his death, and Jack had gone to live in Spain. He'd been terrified of a prison sentence. But over the years he'd managed to get away for a few days every year, drive through France, sail across the Channel and visit Martha. It seemed their love for each other had endured and grown stronger despite their separation.

Sarah put the letters down and thought about what she'd read. It was in the seventies that she'd visited Aunt Martha. Jack had still been alive then. *My private place to be with Jack*. So this was where they'd met and spent time together. Maybe Jack had even been here when Sarah had visited. *Don't open the door!*

The last letter was dated 1980. In it, Jack wrote of his battle with cancer.

A minute later, Sarah pulled the curtain across, left the hut and locked the door.

'Sorry, Aunt Martha. You were right,' she whispered. 'I should never have opened the door. And I should never have doubted you.' She went down on to the beach and walked to the water's edge. Taking the key from her pocket she flung it, as far as she could, out to sea. Let Aunt Martha's secrets stay hidden forever.

The End

Aunt Martha's Secrets – Discussion

This story came close to being accepted. In fact, one fiction editor asked for what she described as 'a few tweaks'.

The 'few tweaks' were actually quite substantial. The editor wanted an explanation of why Aunt Martha didn't just go and live in Spain with her husband, and some back story showing why Sarah's parents could believe Martha capable of murder. She also wanted Sarah to keep something from the hut as a memento rather than let it all be lost when the hut was demolished. And finally, as well as adding all that, she wanted me to reduce the overall length from 2000 to 1500 words!

It all seemed a bit of a tall order. Certainly they weren't edits I could do quickly. Twice I started making the changes, but I'd begun writing a novel and by the time I received this rejection I was immersed in the novel, had stopped writing short stories, and my heart just wasn't in it. I ended up losing the potential sale.

Don't follow my example here. If an editor asks for

changes, make them, and you may make the sale. Even if you preferred your story as originally written, write the new version for the editor. You can always keep your original, and use it if you publish a collection of your stories – if you still prefer it to the rewritten version. But generally speaking, editors know best and the rewrite will be better than the original!

On balance I think this story failed because it had too much plot. To fit the editor's requirements it needed to be shorter, but it also needed more explanation for the plot to make sense, and that simply didn't fit in the word-count.

The simpler stories are usually the best ones. Save your complex plots for your novels.

OK, time to go back to successful published stories, and the last story in this little book. It's very different to the last story, as it has a wonderfully simple little plot and a very short word-count. It was snapped up very quickly by *My Weekly*.

Père Noël Pops the Question

I'm half way down the mountain before it occurs to me that she might not say yes. My hat's slipping down over my eyes, and the beard keeps getting in my mouth. And why I thought I'd be able to ski with a pillow stuffed under my jacket and a sack on my back I'll never know. Suddenly, the whole idea of proposing on a ski slope, on Christmas Day while dressed as Santa, is beginning to seem a bit stupid.

I can see Janine further down the slope, waiting on the ledge just off the piste, as we arranged. Her hair is blowing in the breeze, and her purple ski jacket stands out against the pristine snow and bright blue sky. She looks stunning. The whole day is stunning.

She hasn't spotted me yet, but the ski school have.

'Père Noël! Père Noël!' A line of excited French children snake their way down the piste, performing perfect snowplough turns. I stop and give them a cheery wave. Might as well play the part!

'Vous avez des cadeaux, Père Noël?' Presents, they want presents. My French isn't quite up to saying, *No, just one very special present for one very special lady,* so I just attempt a Ho Ho Ho, a parallel turn and another wave of my ski pole, all at once.

Bad idea. My hat falls further over my eyes, and I hit some powder snow. My left ski tip digs in, my right ski goes over my left, and with my ski pole still completing its cheery wave above my head there's no hope.

I tumble head over heels, and end up planting my face in a deep drift. I've bitten my tongue hard in the fall, and can feel a pool of warm blood collecting in my mouth.

It's not nice, but Père Noël has to do what he must do. The French children stand open-mouthed as I pull off my beard and spit a mouthful of blood onto the snow, then adjust my pillow-belly and re-attach a ski.

'Ho ho ho, Joyeux Noël,' I shout, as I gingerly set off again, somewhat slower this time. My words come out garbled – I've bitten my tongue so hard it hurts to talk.

Down the mountain, I see Janine has noticed me. Earlier, I'd told her to ski ahead to this point, while I visited the little boys' room at the top of the chair-lift. That's where I'd emptied the rucksack I'd been carrying (Janine thought it contained an extra jumper and a picnic for later) and togged up as Father Christmas.

I pat the pocket where I've tucked the ring. Thankfully it's still there despite my tumble.

When I reach her, Janine's as open-mouthed as the children were.

'Nick? Is that you? What on earth…'

'Ho ho ho, Merry Chrithtmath,' I try to say.

Janine's not sure whether to laugh or look worried. 'Nick? It is you, isn't it? I saw you fall. Are you ok?'

'Yeth, it'th me. I'm fine!' I tell her. Time to get down on my knees and do the job properly.

I release the catches on my ski bindings, and in one smooth motion step off my skis and kneel in the snow. She'll guess what I'm up to now, I'm sure.

But she laughs. I'm a little disconcerted. Does that mean she'll say no?

'Nick, poor Nick, let me help you up,' she says, shuffling towards me on her skis. I get it, she thinks I've stepped into soft snow and disappeared up to my knees.

'No, no, I'm OK. I'm meant to be like thith,' I tell her. 'I'm on my kneeth.'

'Your what?'

'Kneeth. Thing ith, Janine. There'th thomething I'd like to athk you.'

Janine is still laughing. My tongue is swelling by the second. If I don't get this question out quickly I won't be able to ask it at all and I'll have to think of some other stunt. I draw a deep breath, take out the ring in its little box, and go for it.

'Janine, will you do me the enormouth honour of marrying me?'

She stops laughing. She fixes her eyes on mine, unclips her skis and kneels down in front of me. Her face is an inch from mine as she pulls down my beard, wipes a drop of blood from my lips with her fingers, and whispers, 'Yes, oh yes, Nick.'

We kiss then, a short, sore kiss owing to the state of my mouth, but a long and lingering embrace. We're on our knees in crisp white snow, half way down a French mountain on Christmas Day, under a blue sky and a bright sun. And I'm dressed as Father Christmas.

The French children snake past. Their instructor shouts to me: 'Oui, ou non?'

'Oui!' I shout back. She said yes. *She said Yes!* SHE SAID YES!

The children let out an enormous cheer. Janine turns and waves at them. She looks radiantly happy, and more beautiful than anything I've ever seen.

She's just given me the greatest Christmas present anyone could ever have.

The End

Père Noël Pops the Question – Discussion

Aw, isn't that sweet? Did you smile at the end and maybe say Aw too? Feels like a good last story for the book. It was inspired by a friend from work, who told me how he proposed to his girlfriend in much the same way. I asked his permission to turn his anecdote into a story, of course, and presented him with a copy of the magazine when it was published.

I've used a little bit of French in the story. It's OK to do this as long as someone knowing not a word of the language can still understand it. So when the ski-children ask for 'cadeaux' I have Nick instantly translate for us, 'presents, they want presents now'. My French is appalling but I checked the bits used here with a friend who speaks it well. And I had to look up how to put in all those pesky accents, especially in words like Père Noël. Which leads nicely on to the next topic I want to discuss.

Proof-reading

After you've written and edited your story, but before you submit it, proof-read it. Go through it one last time, very carefully, looking at every word. Correct spellings and punctuation. Don't rely on spell-check which doesn't know whether you meant bear or bare, wood or would, Carol or Clare. Remove double spaces. Add any missing accents. Make your manuscript as clean and error free as you possibly can. Small errors won't get in the way of a sale, and of course the magazine staff will re-edit the story themselves before publication, but the better your story looks the more professional you'll seem.

And who knows, at some point in the future you

might decide to self-publish a collection of your stories. You'll need to ensure they're thoroughly edited at that stage – either by doing it yourself or paying someone else to do it (unless you've got some very good writer friends!) So get into the habit now of giving everything you complete a thorough and careful proof-read before submission. Don't skimp on this stage.

Writing Prompts

I hope you're now itching to write a women's magazine short story! To help you get started, here are some prompts which might just spark a story idea. If you work better with deadlines, set yourself a kitchen timer for ten minutes, and see if you can come up with the start of a story using one or more of these prompts, in that time. If you don't like the stress of a deadline, then relax, close your eyes and let yourself daydream a story from one of these prompts.

Or just copy out the prompt, write the first thing which comes into your head related to it, and then just carry on scribbling or typing and see where it leads you.

If it goes nowhere, don't worry. It was a warm-up. Don't throw anything you've written away, ever. *Ever.* If you look at it again a month later, it just might spark some new ideas, or there might be a paragraph or a phrase you like and can reuse.

Titles

Write a story to fit one of these possible titles. You can always change the title afterwards if the story has veered off in another direction.

- If At First You Don't Succeed
- Daddy's Girl
- Mrs Fix-It
- Tea And Tambourines
- Dance The Night Away
- Marriage and Mountains
- Love Me Do
- A Direct Hit
- Somewhere Over The Sea
- Once Upon A Time In Berlin
- Yellow Roses
- Separate Lives

First Lines

Use one of these as the first line to get yourself started. When you've completed the story, you can always ditch or change the first line if necessary.

- I wondered who the girl in the red coat could be.
- 'Sharon! Get yourself downstairs this minute!'
- It was just as well the moon was full that night.
- If ever there was a moment when Flo realised she was in love, this was it.
- 'It's now or never,' Jack said. 'We can't go on as we are.'
- Once, there were two sisters. Now, there were three, and as everyone knows, three's a crowd.
- It was in his blood, and he had the scars to prove it.
- The box was battered and broken, and contained exactly what I needed to prove who I really was.
- Why, oh why had Gemma left her diary out on her desk?
- If I didn't get the promotion this time, I swore I'd leave.
- It may have been normal in times of war, but we were supposed to be at peace.
- 'Are the drugs working?' Leslie asked. I didn't know how to answer him.

Songs as prompts

Use these song titles as inspiration. Or use the lyrics for these songs, or any other favourite song. You can look up the lyrics on websites such as www.lyrics.com or www.songlyrics.com. Unfortunately I'd fall foul of copyright laws if I included even just one line of a song in this book, so all I can suggest as prompts are the titles (there's no copyright on titles). (You might like to try guessing which of these are from my iPod playlist and which were suggested by my teenage son.)

- Shine on you crazy diamond (Pink Floyd)
- On the bright side of the road (Van Morrison)
- Love song to a stranger (Joan Baez)
- If I had you (Adam Lambert)
- Misery business (Paramore)
- That's what you get (Paramore)
- Perfect ten (Beautiful South)
- Here's to never growing up (Avril Lavigne)
- What do you want from me (Pink Floyd)
- Somewhere only we know (Keane)
- You give love a bad name (Bon Jovi)
- Somewhere over the rainbow (Vera Lynn)
- A rainy night in Soho (Pogues)

Single word prompts

What's the first thing which comes into your head when you think of these words? Discard that. What's the second thing? What's the third thing? Write a story using the *third* idea. I did this with my story *On the Road to Katmandu*. The prompt was 'dust'. I first thought of the state of my mantelpiece – desperately in need of contact with a duster. I then thought of the horrors of DIY building dust – especially the type you get when you drill into breezeblocks. And thirdly, I remembered the choking pre-Monsoon dust I'd experienced on that bus in Nepal.

- Dust
- Freedom
- Spring
- Inheritance
- Spider
- Loneliness
- Found
- Excuse
- Mission
- Connection
- Final
- College

Longer prompts

If the single words don't work for you, try using short phrases. If you have a poetry book to hand, pick out a line or a phrase as inspiration. I've made these up just now – I'm sure you could do better. Try spending an afternoon writing or compiling prompts lists which you can use for future writing sessions.

- blue Tuesday
- from melon to lemon
- pay it forward
- a carton of cats
- not the hat, never the hat
- a lift from Long Island
- group gratitude
- because it's there
- the weeping violin
- the perfect fifth
- down the plain lane
- when the child cries

Structure

Try writing a story with an unusual structure. Pick a structure and write your story around it. Here are a few ideas or come up with your own.

- A story in four sections, each section is a different season
- Traffic lights – red, amber, green
- Entries from a diary
- Entries from a diary, going backwards in time
- A to-do list
- A recipe – let the story ingredients combine and cook along with the recipe
- Five sections – four fingers and a thumb
- Two weddings and a christening
- A story which covers a lot of time – following a child maturing or a tree growing
- The three trimesters of pregnancy, or three school terms
- Six nations, or five continents, or two hemispheres
- Stages in the building of a house

Proverbs and Sayings

Take a well known proverb or saying such as the ones below, and write a story to illustrate it.

- Too many cooks spoil the broth
- The early bird catches the worm
- He who hesitates is lost
- Money makes the world go round
- Love is always open arms
- Time and tide wait for no man
- Small ones are more juicy
- Say it with flowers
- Look before you leap
- Many hands make light work
- Money isn't everything
- Blood is thicker than water

Picture Prompts

Save photos from Sunday supplements or other magazines as prompts. Or take a look at the pictures used to illustrate womag stories, and write a *different* story to fit the picture.

Well, that little lot should keep you going! Having a notebook full of story ideas means that whenever you've got time to write, you won't be short of prompts to get you started.

In Conclusion

That brings us to the end of this book. I hope you've enjoyed the stories, and that you've learned from or been inspired by the discussions. I think the only thing left is for me to provide you with a quick summary – things to think about when writing a womag story. So here it is for quick and easy reference.

1. Get ideas from anywhere and everywhere. If an idea isn't enough on its own, combine it with another.

2. Ensure your story has a beginning, a middle, an end, and a *point* to make.

3. Remember the comedy story arc, and give your readers a happy or hopeful ending.

4. Decide where in the emotional scale you are pitching your story – funny, sweet, emotional – and write accordingly.

5. Good characterisation is essential. Your main character must be someone the reader likes, and can relate to.

6. Consider having an unusual setting – it'll help make the story stand out.

7. Always include some dialogue. Give your characters different voices which suit their age and personality.

8. Include description, but make it do more than one job.

9. Add a twist ending if you can think of one, but make sure the story works as well without it.

10. If you're stuck on a story, get other writers to take a look. Something they say might spark a new idea.

11. Check your facts – all of them – and get them right.

12. Edit and proof-read your story and correct all errors.

13. Research your market. Read the magazines you are submitting to, and send them the kind of thing they regularly publish.

14. If you're short of writing time, prioritise writing and make everything else fit around it. And give up ironing – no one will notice.

If you sell a story inspired by reading this book, do let me know! I can be contacted via my website www.kathleenmcgurl.com or my 'womagwriter' blog www.womagwriter.blogspot.co.uk . I always love to hear from other writers.

Good luck and happy writing!

Further Reading

How to Write and Sell Short Stories by Della Galton – the queen of womag fiction takes you through the process from start to finish. Accent Press.

The Short Story Writer's Toolshed by Della Galton – a snappy no-nonsense guide to the art of writing stories. Soundhaven Publishing.

Monkeys with Typewriters by Scarlett Thomas – an in-depth look at the power of fiction and the structure of stories. Canongate Books.

Secrets and Rain by Cally Taylor – a collection of published and award-wining short stories which will warm your heart. KDP Publishing.

Tears and Laughter and Happy Ever After – a collection of 26 short stories by various womag writers. Blot Publishing.

Diamonds and Pearls – another collection of women's magazine short stories, with a percentage of each sale going to a breast cancer charity. Accent Press.

Short Circuit: A Guide to the Art of the Short Story (ed Vanessa Gebbie) – a collection of essays about the art and craft of short story writing. Salt Publishing.

Back to Creative Writing School by Bridget Whelan – a superb book of inspiring writing exercises to get your creative juices flowing. KDP Publishing

Acknowledgements

My sincere thanks to Pauline Higgins and Jean Buswell, who read and commented on the first edition of this book.

Thanks too to Della Galton for being an ever-inspiring writing teacher.

I should also include a nod to my gorgeous husband, Ignatius McGurl, for his inspiring thoughts on how to find time to write.

And of course, thanks as always to the wonderful Write Women. Without you lovely lot I'd have given up writing years ago. The value of your friendship and support is immeasurable.

About the Author

Kathleen McGurl lives in Bournemouth with her husband and younger son, her elder son having flown the nest. She always wanted to write, and for many years was waiting until she had the time.

Eventually she came to the bitter realisation no one would pay her for a year off work to write a book, so she sat down and started to write one anyway. Since then she has sold dozens of short stories to women's magazines. These days she is concentrating on longer fiction, and is currently trying to find an agent for her full-length time-slip novel, while also writing another in the same genre.

She works full time in the IT industry and when she's not writing, she's often out running, slowly.

Ghost Stories and How to Write Them
by Kathleen McGurl

If you've ever wanted to write a ghost story that will sell to UK women's magazines, this is the book for you. It contains a dozen stories, most of which have been previously published in the womags, and takes you through what makes a good, gentle ghost story for this market.

27895580R00093

Made in the USA
Charleston, SC
25 March 2014